G000092774

Chase Down

A Detective Ryan Chase Thriller, Volume 2

M K Farrar

Published by Warwick House Press, 2021.

Chapter One

The LED lights of the digital clock flipped over to 3:00 a.m., and the snick of a catch opening was barely audible in the still house.

In the bedrooms, the others slept on, unaware. Even the familiar creak of a floorboard as a foot pressed upon it didn't alert them to the fact that they weren't alone.

He wasn't overly worried about the noise. It was unlikely it would wake any of them. Even so, he'd taken precautions. The windows had internal latches, but he'd made sure to lock them and hide the keys. It was a cool night, so there shouldn't have been any reason for the family to want the windows open and notice them missing. A chair wedged beneath a handle would prevent the doors being opened should someone wake.

He stopped at the bedroom of the two adults. The steady breathing of the woman and the louder snore of the man vibrated through the air. How could she sleep with that going on? Of course, tonight he was far less likely to disturb her slumber.

The weight of the knife felt good in his hand, like it belonged there, an extension of who he was. He had planned for this moment, but that didn't change the conflicting swirl of emotions inside him. Things could have been so different. The wedge of disappointment had grown deeper day by day, and now it seemed to be splitting him open, like an axe inside a thick log.

Carefully, he edged open the bedroom door. A crack from between the curtains allowed light to spill in from the street outside. City living meant it was never fully dark, or quiet. There were always people around, cars driving by, alarms going off. He liked that about living here. It meant someone moving around in the middle of the night was rarely noticed.

The two sleeping forms of the adults lay lumped under the bedcovers. The woman faced the window, her dark hair partially hiding her face. The man lay on his back, his hands folded over his chest in a pose that was strangely reminiscent of someone in a coffin. He couldn't help but smile at that thought. Had the man somehow predicted what was about to happen to him and had taken up the position? It didn't help with the snoring, his mouth open, chin hanging slack.

He switched hands with the knife. He wore gloves, so as not to leave any prints, and had a swim cap over his hair. He probably looked ridiculous, but he didn't care about that. Anyone who was going to see him would be dead moments later, and he doubted they'd be worried about his appearance. They'd be more concerned about their loved ones, fearful of the same fate meeting them, which it would. He'd done his research. He had no intention of getting caught. No prints, no strands of hair left behind. He'd be sure not to leave his saliva anywhere either. And as for semen, he pulled a face in disgust. He was no pervert, and he wouldn't have such a thing said about him either.

He needed to deal with the man first. That would be his biggest potential problem. If he didn't work fast and be decisive, things could go wrong, and he couldn't afford for that to happen.

He approached the bed and folded both hands around the hilt of the knife, one above the other, the blade pointing down. Still, no one showed any sign of being aware of his presence, their breathing remaining steady.

This *perfect* family, and this *perfect* home. It was all a lie. He knew that. Now others would, too.

He angled himself over the bed, the sharp point of the blade quivering mere inches from the man's face. Excitement bubbled up through him, and he forced himself to take a calming breath. Once he put events into motion, there would be no going back, and he needed to keep his wits about him.

The man's eyes blinked open.

Without another thought, he swung the knife, angling the blade so it punctured one of the man's eyeballs, forcing the blade up into the brain. The man barely had a second to react, a strangled breath, a gasp of shock. His body stiffened as though a bolt of electricity had gone through him, his feet thrashing, before the lights went out forever.

Beside him, the woman gave a small moan and shifted in her sleep. He'd done everything he could to try to prevent her waking, but it might not have been enough. The thrashing had been more than he'd anticipated, and now maybe her subconscious had alerted her to there being something wrong.

She lifted her head, and muttered, but hadn't yet turned his way. He froze, his heart knocking against the cage of his ribs. He held in a squeal of excitement, reining himself in. Did he hold still and hope she went back to sleep, or did he risk making more noise by yanking the knife out of the man's eye socket?

If he was going to continue with his plan, he was going to have to do it at some point.

Bunching his muscles and gritting his teeth, he pulled at the knife. The noise and sensation of metal against bone did something strange to his teeth, hurting them down to the roots.

The woman must have heard something as she rolled to face him just as the knife came free, the blade almost black with blood in the poor light.

Her eyes sprang open, and she let out a shriek and threw herself backwards, falling out of bed. She got caught up in the duvet, so her legs were still tangled on the mattress, her bottom and hands now on the floor.

He didn't waste any more time. He rounded the bed, the knife brandished in one hand.

She opened her mouth and screamed.

He was more worried about the neighbours hearing something than the reaction of those left in the house. If they'd heard that scream, they might realise something was up and call the police. He'd been able to plan for those within the house, but not those outside of these walls. The property was terraced and so was attached to neighbours on both sides. He'd have preferred the place to be detached, but he couldn't help that.

He leaned down and grabbed her hair in his fist, holding her steady. She lashed out at him, battering him with her fists. She tried to kick, but her legs were still covered in the padding of the duvet, and she only succeeded in getting herself more tangled. He wrenched her head back by her hair and brought the blade in a decisive line across her throat. Her body bucked, and hot blood spurted across his face. Damn it. That was a mess. He would have liked to avoid a mess, but he guessed it couldn't be helped.

Beneath him, the woman gurgled, the same kind of noise her husband had made, but she seemed unaware of where she was or what was happening to her.

He stood over her and waited. It took longer this time. Her body bleeding out, the light gradually dimming from her eyes. He wished he could hear what was going on in her head. What were her final thoughts? Was she thinking of her daughter in the other room and praying the girl wouldn't be next? Or was the fear of dying even greater than the love for her offspring?

Finally, her struggles slowed, and she slumped and fell still, her jaw slack, her chest a dark apron of blood. It had soaked into the carpet beneath her and spattered across the walls and the bed, but he didn't care. It wasn't as though he'd be cleaning up the room.

Banging came from the room across the landing, but he'd taken precautions. She wouldn't get out.

He left the parents' bedroom and stepped out onto the landing. He rolled his neck and shoulders, loosening the muscles, the knife dangling from his hand at his side. His gaze alit on the closed bedroom door and the chair propped beneath the handle.

She was next.

Chapter Two

The street in Bedminster, Bristol, looked like so many others in the area. A row of terraced Victorian houses stood on both sides, the pavement bordered by cars parked bumper to bumper. Those same cars were now blocked from leaving by a couple of police response vans at either end. It was four-thirty on Monday afternoon, and residents returning from work discovered themselves unable to drive down their road.

DI Ryan Chase had stopped outside the outer cordon and walked the rest, ducking under the inner cordon and flashing his ID at the officers. More marked police cars were in the middle of the street, blocking the way.

Neighbours held one another, sobbing into each other's arms, or staring, pale-faced at the scene before them, anxiously chewing their nails, in shock that something so terrible could happen in their own neighbourhood. The realisation it could have been them, *their* families who'd been brutally slaughtered in their beds, had hit them hard.

Ryan spotted the police sergeant coordinating the scene. She was talking to a couple of other officers, so he walked over to join her.

Sergeant Laura Frome was a severe-looking woman in her fifties, her hair bleached so blonde it was almost white and pulled back from her face in a French braid.

"Ah, DI Chase, you're here. Terrible business," she said, her lips pinched tight. "Who would do such a thing?"

An ordinary neighbourhood in Bristol had become the scene of a shockingly violent multiple murder, including a teenager and a young girl.

"That's what we're here to find out," Ryan said. "What have you got so far?"

"Four bodies. Two adults and two children, a boy and a girl, aged sixteen and eleven respectively. We haven't had an official ID done yet, but according to friends and neighbours, they are Hugh and Liz Wyndham, and the kids are Sheldon and Dulcie. The alarm was raised by a friend of the family, thirty-seven-year-old Alison Perry. Dulcie never showed up at school today. The school had phoned the mobile numbers they had on record for both parents, but both phones went straight through to answerphone. When neither the child nor parents still hadn't shown up by the end of school, Mrs Perry decided to pop round and noticed all the curtains were drawn in the house, which was unusual for that time of day. She tried shouting through the letter box, and still didn't get an answer. She trusted her instinct that something was wrong and called the police. Uniformed officers gained access to the property and discovered the bodies in each of the bedrooms."

"The house was locked from the inside?" Ryan asked.

"That's right, and they had a house alarm armed that went off when the officers gained access. There was no break-in, at least not that we can see anyway. No broken windows, no forced locks, or anything like that."

"And the alarm was set? Could it be a murder-suicide?"

"Possibly, but you're going to need to take a look at the scene. There are a few things that don't quite add up."

Movement farther down the street caught his attention, and he turned as his partner, DS Mallory Lawson, strode towards them.

Sorry, she mouthed at him—an apology for being late. She'd texted him earlier to explain that she'd been having problems with her brother, Oliver. He'd been having nightmares ever since he'd accidentally started a small fire in their kitchen, and even though that had been several months ago now, it didn't seem as though he was going to get over it quickly.

"This is my partner, DS Lawson," he introduced to the sergeant.

Frome stuck out her hand. "Laura Frome," she said, and Mallory returned the handshake.

Ryan quickly brought Mallory up to speed.

She shook her head. "That poor family."

"I know," Ryan agreed. "The city is going to the dogs."

On the drive over, Ryan had noted the number of shops with metal shutters pulled down over the storefronts, graffiti scribbled across them. With the exception of the wealthier areas like Clifton, much of the city seemed to be on a decline. This latest incident only helped to confirm that.

Frome continued. "The mother, Liz Wyndham, sent a text to her friend, Alison Perry, last night at nine-forty, so we're assuming the family were all right then. Whoever did this must have committed the murders sometime during the night."

"What did the text say?" Mallory asked.

"Just that she was tired and couldn't believe it was almost Monday already." Frome shrugged. "Doesn't seem to be anything important. I've got my officers going door to door interviewing each of the neighbours to find out if any of them saw or heard anything."

Ryan nodded. "Can your team find out if any of the neighbours have home security as well?"

"Of course."

The increasing use of things like 'Ring' doorbells that had cameras in them was growing and could prove to be handy in cases like these. He glanced up at the red alarm box attached to the outside of the house.

"It's a shame the family didn't have CCTV as well as the home security." Ryan looked down the congested street. "Let's check each of these cars as well, make sure they each belong to the residents, and there isn't one that's out of place."

He spotted the coroner's car among them.

"Who's the attending coroner?" He tried to sound casual.

"Nikki Francis," Frome said.

Ryan tried to ignore the slight uptick of his pulse. He hadn't had too much to do with Nikki since he'd walked out on her on their one disastrous date that summer. The memory of it still made him cringe. They'd exchanged a few work emails since then but had kept it professional. Their paths had crossed a couple of times, but he'd sent Mallory down to speak to her, if he could. It wasn't something he was proud of.

"Okay, let's go inside."

Ryan approached the house, he and Mallory pulling on protective outerwear as they went. A uniformed officer guarded the scene, and Ryan offered him a nod as they passed.

It was important to have as few people in the house as possible, preventing any contamination of the crime scene.

The front door already stood open, revealing the original Victorian tiled floor, combined with duck-egg blue walls. SOCO were busy at work, dusting for prints, and footprints, and checking for any signs of blood.

Ryan entered the hallway and popped his head into the living room briefly. The bay window offered a view onto the street and the medley of people beyond. The place was tastefully decorated, spacious with high ceilings and original cornices. A paperback, that would never get finished, lay open on the arm of the cream sofa, and a games console sat beneath the stand for the flat-screen television. There were no signs of violence in the room. Someone could walk through this house and be completely unaware of the tragedy that had occurred upstairs.

Ryan left the living room and followed Frome up the stairs, Mallory close behind.

"The master bedroom is straight ahead," Frome said, "and is where both bodies of the two adults were found. The middle room is the teenage son's bedroom, and the box room at the end belonged to the daughter. All four were found in their rooms. Let's take a look at the adults first."

Ryan entered the master bedroom to discover someone was already there. Even beneath the protective clothing, Ryan recognised the blonde hair, blue eyes, and glasses of Nikki Francis.

Nikki noticed she had company and straightened from where she'd been leaning over the body of Hugh Wyndham.

"Hello, Ryan," she said. "Long time no see."

He was battling between being pleased to see her and trying not to drown in his own awkwardness. "Nikki, how are you?"

She nodded. "Good, busy with work."

"People just keep on dying," he said, using what he hoped she'd take as humour to hide his discomfort.

"I guess it's good for business," she threw back.

An outsider might raise an eyebrow at their conversation, especially considering the gravity of the situation, but sometimes it felt like the only way to stop himself from going crazy. He still sensed a flirtation between them, a lingering eye contact, their close proximity. There was the potential for a relationship, if only he could get a hold of his issues, but he didn't want to risk work colleagues finding out about his OCD. He prided himself in his ability to do his job—it was the one thing he had left after losing his daughter and his marriage breaking down—and he didn't want to screw that up as well. He thought that Mallory had an inkling that all wasn't quite right with him, but she was the person he was closest to, and he trusted that she'd keep her mouth shut, unless she thought it was affecting his ability to do his job.

Mallory cleared her throat, and Ryan caught her throwing him a wide-eyed stare.

He pulled himself back to professional mode. "So, what are your thoughts?" he asked Nikki.

"Obviously, I'll be able to tell more once we get the bodies down to the mortuary, but all four members were stabbed, which is most likely the cause of death. The father was stabbed through the left eye socket, causing a massive brain injury. The wife had her throat cut, and it caught the carotid artery, as you can tell from the arc of the blood spatter across the wall and curtains."

The woman was half on, half off the bed. The blood had turned dark and sticky, indicating several hours had passed since it had been spilled.

"Whoever cut her throat would have been covered in her blood," Ryan said.

She nodded in agreement. "Yes, I'd say it would have been near impossible to avoid."

"Can you tell which of them was killed first?"

"At a guess, I'd say the man, purely because he doesn't appear to have moved from the position he was sleeping in. The woman looks as though she was trying to escape, so she must have seen or heard what was happening to her husband and tried to get away. Unfortunately, she didn't get very far."

"They didn't hear the person coming in?"

"Doesn't seem that way."

Ryan took a moment, assessing the rest of the room. There was nothing to suggest this was a burglary gone wrong—no drawers or cupboards had been opened, and the jewellery box on the vanity table remained closed, too. Both the victims had a glass of water sitting on the bedside tables next to them. The woman's side also had a Kindle.

He noticed something. "Where are their phones?"

"Not here," Frome said. "We haven't seen any sign of any mobile phones in any of the rooms."

"But didn't the school try to call the parents? And the deceased had texted her friend the night before. If they didn't have mobile phones, what was she texting on?"

"You think someone took them?"

He twisted his lips. "That's my assumption but it doesn't look like a burglary. Why take the phones, and nothing else?"

No one could come up with an answer.

"Show me the children," he said.

This was the worst part of his job, by far. Adults, he could deal with, no matter how violent or tragic the deaths, but kids triggered him, taking him back to the days when he'd first lost his daughter.

They went to the box room first. Ryan exhaled slowly through his nose and then stepped inside. He almost couldn't bring himself to look, but he knew he had to. This girl deserved to have a detective who was willing to really see her to work out what had happened, no matter how hard.

If his own daughter, Hayley, had lived, she'd have been around this girl's age now.

He took a shaky breath and swallowed against the painful knot constricting his throat and turned his face so his colleagues wouldn't see how badly the girl's death affected him.

Dulcie Wyndham was slumped against the chest of drawers, a streak of blood running down the painted wood where she must have slid down. Her hair hung over her face, and for that Ryan was grateful. She was in a t-shirt and a pair of cotton shorts, which she must have worn to bed, the items now dark with blood.

"She has several knife wounds to the chest," Nikki said. "No obvious signs of a struggle or that she fought back."

Ryan shook his head in dismay. "Jesus, poor kid. She must have heard something going on in her parents' room. Did she try and hide in here? Why didn't she run?"

"Maybe because she knew her attacker?" Mallory suggested.

Ryan exhaled. "Let's see the boy."

He stepped out of the room onto the landing. A chair outside the door gave him reason to pause. He checked the wood underneath the door handle on the outside.

"Someone barricaded her in here," he said. "They were worried she'd wake up and raise the alarm. They planned this, knew which order they were going to kill each of the family members in. This was definitely premeditated."

"I hate to say it, but don't think we can rule out the teenager," Frome said. "We found the knife still in his body, so he was clearly the final victim. The big question is if it was self-inflicted or if someone else stabbed him. He has a lot of blood over him—more than I'd expect just from a single stab wound. It could be the blood of his sister and mother."

"Show me."

Ryan walked into the boy's room. The walls were covered in posters for heavy metal bands and classic slasher horror films. The bedcovers were black, as were the curtains. The room wouldn't have been out of place in a horror flick anyway, but the body of the sixteen-year-old lying in a pool of blood in the middle of the carpet gave it added weight. Sticking out of his stomach was a large kitchen knife.

"We have to consider that this knife is the murder weapon," Ryan said, standing over him.

Frome nodded. "Looks to be that way, as far as we can tell. Nothing else has been found in the house. Obviously, forensics will give us a better idea."

Ryan turned to Nikki. "Is whether he did it himself or not something you can determine during the post-mortem?"

"I might be able to get an idea either way, depending on the angle of the blade and the depth of the wound, but it won't determine it for sure."

Ryan blew out a breath. "With all the doors locked and no sign of a break-in, it does seem as though the attack came from inside the house. I don't think we can ignore how this looks."

Frome raised an eyebrow. "That he killed his parents and sister, and then stabbed himself in the stomach?"

"The most obvious explanation is normally the right one," Ryan said, "but until we get forensics back, we'll need to keep our minds open."

Ryan stepped outside of the room again, back onto the landing. He ducked at the door and checked beneath the handle. "Do you see this?" he said to Mallory.

She dropped down to get a better view. "Scrapes against the metal and wood?"

Ryan nodded. "They're the same as beneath the girl's door."

"You think someone jammed a chair under his door handle as well?"

"I'd say so. Unfortunately, it's impossible to say when that happened. Maybe the parents used it as a way of keeping him in his room, and he replicated it to keep his sister from running away."

"There might have been abuse in the home," Mallory suggested. "Perhaps that's the motive the boy had for killing his parents?"

"But then why kill the sister as well?" he said. "If she was suffering from the same abuse, what motive would he have to murder her?"

She shrugged. "He just snapped. It does happen."

Ryan agreed, it did, but it was too soon to make any judgements for sure. They'd need to interview any remaining family, plus friends, and the teachers at school, find out if there had been any signs of abuse on the children.

"Until we get forensic results from the blood on the body and prints from the knife, we don't know what happened. Just 'cause a kid's got a black bedcover doesn't make him capable of murdering his family."

Mallory straightened and put her hands on her hips. "The doors were all locked from the inside, the alarm was set. It's more likely than not that someone from inside the house killed them all, and since he was clearly the last one to die..."

"I understand your thinking but like I said, let's wait for forensics and the post-mortem before we jump to any conclusions."

A shout came from downstairs. "We've found something."

Ryan exchanged a glance with Mallory, and they both hurried back to the ground floor. The shout had come from the kitchen, so Ryan went in to find one of the Scenes of Crime officers holding up a freezer bag containing what appeared to be four mobile phones.

"Guess we've found the phones," Mallory said.

Ryan narrowed his eyes. "That's odd. Why would the family's mobile phones be in the freezer?"

The officer handed the bag over to Ryan, and he held them up to eye level. "They're all switched off."

"Maybe someone put them there to hide them?" Mallory said. "Hid them from the family members so they couldn't put a call in for help?"

"And if they were switched off, they wouldn't be able to call the phones to locate them either." Ryan contemplated these most recent findings. "What's the last thing you do before you go to bed, Mallory?"

"Umm, check my phone. Make sure my alarm is set."

"Yep, same. Someone must have gathered up the phones while the family was sleeping. If they'd done it before then, the owners would have noticed they were missing, and known something was wrong."

She tilted her head slightly. "So, someone moved around the house while they were asleep and took the phones? How did this person know where they'd all be?"

"Where do you keep yours at night?"

"On my nightstand, beside my bed."

"Whoever did this wouldn't have wanted the victims to have such easy access to their mobile phones, so they took them, turned them off, and hid them."

"They weren't worried about being seen?"

"Maybe they thought it was worth the risk." Ryan turned to Ben Glazier, who was the Scenes of Crime coordinator. "Have you found anything else down here?"

He shook his head. "Not yet."

"No blood?"

"Not that we've found."

"Then it was contained to the upstairs." He wondered out loud. "If someone murdered four people, wouldn't they have blood on them? On their shoes, or their hands. What would the chances be of them being able to walk through a house to leave without getting some of that blood on the floors or walls or doors?"

Mallory grimaced. "Slim to none."

"Exactly. So, what happened? Were they wearing a getup like this?" He gestured to their own protective gear, "and disposed of it upstairs? If so, where is it?"

"Or they took it with them?"

"Yes, also a possibility, but it must mean they took the time to clean up. Most people, if they were to break into a house and murder four people, would want to get out again as quickly as possible, but this person must have taken the time to make sure they didn't have blood on them."

"Or it was the son," Mallory pointed out. "He would have been able to move around the house freely and would know where each family member kept their phone at night. It would also explain why there is no blood downstairs because none of them ever came downstairs. They all died in their rooms, including him."

Ryan pointed a finger at her. "But then why did he hide his own phone in the freezer? What would be the point? It's not as though he wouldn't know where he put it."

"He didn't want one of his family members to get hold of it and call for help? Or else he was trying to make it appear as though he was just a victim, too?"

"Good suggestions, but he hasn't made any other attempt to make it look as though he wasn't the one responsible for the murders. If he was trying to make it appear as though someone had broken in, wouldn't he have at least unlocked the door and disabled the alarm? I bet he would have known the code."

They left the house again, and Ryan stepped back to get a view of the front wall. The alarm system bothered him.

Sergeant Frome joined them, and Ryan pointed at the small red box on the side of the house.

"Why do they have an alarm system? Were they just paranoid? Had they been broken into before?"

Frome checked her notes. "There's a police report from a couple of months ago where the wife claimed someone was watching the house. Police came out, couldn't see anything, but they suggested she put the alarm system in."

"If someone else has the alarm code and a key, they could have let themselves into the house, disabled the alarm, murdered the family, and then got out again, resetting the alarm and locking the door behind them "

Frome raised her eyebrows. "Sounds like someone who knew them then, for them to know the codes."

"Or no one broke into the house in the first place," Mallory interjected, "and it was the teenage son who was responsible."

Ryan mused on the possibility. "We need to contact the alarm company and get a record of when the alarm was armed and disabled. That should give us a better idea about who entered and left the house, and at what time."

He assumed the family didn't normally set and unset the alarm in the middle of the night, and so it would be out of place on the history. Would that mean it was someone close to the family who would have access to that information, though? Maybe someone who worked for the alarm company would also know. He didn't know enough about how house alarms worked, so he jotted down in his notebook quickly to get one of his constables to check it out.

Movement came from the front door, and Ryan glanced over as Nikki exited the property.

She pulled down the hood of her protective wear and removed her gloves and mask. "I assume we'll talk again once the post-mortems have been done," she said to Ryan.

"Yes, absolutely. I'm particularly interested to get your thoughts on the boy's stab wound."

"I'll give you my thoughts, but I won't be able to tell one hundred percent either way. It's up to you to come to a conclusion."

"Of course. I just trust your opinion."

She paused for a moment, her gaze fixed on his face, her lips slightly pursed. "You know, it's a shame it's taken a murdered family to get to see you again."

Heat rose to his face. "Sorry, life's been a bit crazy."

She shrugged. "Sure, you don't have to make excuses."

"No, really. My wife—" he corrected himself, realising his mistake, "my ex-wife—has cancer. I've been helping out where I can."

She grimaced. "Oh, shit, sorry. I didn't mean to be an arsehole about it."

He immediately felt bad for using Donna's illness as an excuse about why he'd been avoiding her. "No, I should be sorry. I'm the arsehole."

She gave a small smile. "You're helping your ex-wife when she has cancer. That doesn't sound like such a bad thing to me."

"Maybe not. The new guy buggered off the minute she got the diagnosis and left her on her own. I didn't feel like I could do the same."

"I understand."

She didn't, though, and that wasn't her fault. He'd never confided in her, or anyone else for that matter, about the struggles he went through every day. He convinced himself it was no one else's business when, really, he was worried about the repercussions of letting people in. He didn't want to be given all the well-meaning advice about what to do, even by people who cared about him and meant well.

"Detective," Sergeant Frome called him over. "One of the neighbours might have heard something."

Ryan was glad to have the distraction.

"Excuse me," he said to Nikki. "Work calls."

She nodded in understanding. "I'll give you a call when I'm done with the post-mortems."

"See you then."

He was relieved that their next meeting would take place in the mortuary. No one could get any wrong ideas when they were standing over a body that had been opened from groin to sternum during an autopsy.

Chapter Three

Helen Bolton stared at the chopping board and knife abandoned on the worksurface, and a familiar feeling of irritation rose inside her, spilling out of her mouth.

"How many times do I have to ask you to clean up after yourself?" She grabbed the items, throwing them into the dishwasher, and then angrily running water over a cloth to wipe down the surface again. "We've got an estate agent arriving any minute now, and despite the house looking perfect when I left for work this morning, you seem to have managed to trash it since you got home."

From the kitchen table, her fifteen-year-old daughter, Reese, rolled her eyes. "Oh my God, Mum, you're so overreacting. I do live here, remember? I was hungry when I got back from school, so I got a snack."

"I don't care if you got a snack, I care if you left everything all over the kitchen worktop. Haven't you ever heard of a dishcloth?"

Reese pouted and slid down in her chair. "I don't even want to sell the house. What's wrong with where we are?"

Helen let out a long sigh. "I'm not having this conversation with you again. Your dad's job has moved, and we can't ask him to commute for almost three hours a day to get there and back. It's not fair on him."

"What about what's fair on us? All our friends are here."

"You'll still be able to see them. Exeter isn't that far away."

"If it's not that far, why can't Dad commute?"

"It's a bit different when we're talking about your social life versus the thing that's keeping a roof over our heads and food in our stomachs."

She really didn't have time to go over all this again. She understood it was hard for the kids to have to change cities and schools, but that was just what had to happen, and they would adapt.

Reese shoved back her chair with all the grace of a two-year-old throwing a temper tantrum. "Ugh, whatever. I'm going to my room. I've got homework to do."

Helen held back a scream. Why did Reese have to be so bloody unreasonable all the time? Why was it so hard for her to put something away after she'd used it or wipe down a surface? Helen missed when her daughter had been small—not that Reese's younger brother, Tyler, was much better. He was twelve now and almost as moody as his sister. She was surprised her husband, Andy, even wanted them to move to be closer to his work. At the moment, he got to be out of the house twelve hours a day and by the time he got back, she'd already dealt with all the chaos of the time between the end of school and after dinner. He got to come home and put his feet up. Not that she resented him for it—well, not *all* the time anyway. Things would change once they'd moved, and he was able to drive to and from work within half an hour. He'd be here more, and she could leave him to deal with the kids' bad tempers.

She finished cleaning up Reese's mess and then whizzed around the lounge, plumping cushions and straightening picture frames.

The doorbell went, and she hurried to answer it, smoothing back her hair and hoping she didn't look too flustered. She had to remind herself that these people were working for her, and not the other way around. She hated other people coming into her house, though, always feeling as though it was being judged. She tried her best to keep the place as tidy as possible, but it felt like a never-ending task between work and the kids. She'd thought it had been hard enough when the children had been little, and she'd been forever picking up toys and hoovering crumbs. But they only seemed to have got worse as they'd got older, and now they could help themselves to their own food and yet never seemed to manage to clear up after themselves. They drove her crazy. Maybe she was a bad parent and needed to come down on them harder, but life for a teenager didn't exactly seem easy either. They had so much pressure on them all the time that she hated giving them a tough time at home as well.

Helen opened the door.

An attractive man in his late forties in a suit stood on her doorstep, a tall, younger man standing slightly behind and to one side of him.

"Mrs Bolton," the older of the two said brightly, putting out his hand for her to shake. "James Voysey from Stem and Prince Estate Agents."

She shook his hand. "Yes, hello. Come on in. I've been expecting you."

The two men stepped into the house.

"This is my colleague, Philip Sweeny," James introduced.

She shook his hand, too.

"You have a beautiful home, Mrs Bolton," he said.

"Thank you." She did like this house. It was a modern new build and was surprisingly spacious, but they weren't selling because of the house. It was the location that was no longer working for them.

James agreed with his colleague. "Yes, you do. Thank you for choosing Stem and Prince to market your property. We'll be taking some photographs and also some three-sixty video footage for you today, so we can get everything online hopefully by the end of the week."

It surprised her. "Oh, that soon?"

He flashed her a wide smile. "No reason why not, assuming you're happy to progress with everything. I understand you've priced for a quick sale."

"That's right. My husband has a new job, and he's commuting, and it's not easy, for any of us really. Feels like he's barely here."

"Of course, I completely understand. That must be hard on the family."

"It is, that's why we need to move. We'd thought it might be manageable, but unfortunately it's not." She remembered her manners. "Can I get you anything? Tea? Coffee? Water?"

"No, I'm fine thanks." He turned to the younger man. "You need anything, Philip?"

"No, but thanks for the offer."

She smiled at him. He really was very tall—at least six feet three or even four. She assumed he was the photographer, since he carried equipment with him.

"I'll just let you get on with it then," she said, feeling awkward. "Oh, and my kids are in their rooms. Just tell them to step out for a minute while you do the photos." She hesitated. "On second thought, I'll make them go and sit in the garden."

She also wanted to make sure they hadn't sneaked any bowls or cups up there while her back had been turned, or that one of them would have left their dirty underwear out in plain sight for the estate agents to deal with.

"We'll get started down here," James Voysey said. He jerked his chin at his colleague. "That work all right with you?"

Philip shrugged as though he was already bored. "Of course."

"Shout if you need anything," Helen said.

She left them to it and sprinted up the stairs.

"Reese? Tyler?" She knocked on her kids' doors. "The estate agents are here. You need to make yourselves scarce." Muttered complaints came from inside both the rooms. "Come on, you two. Don't make me show you up in front of a couple of strangers."

A humph of irritation came from her daughter's room. The door opened, and Reese appeared, scowling in the gap. "This is so unfair. I have homework to do."

"It won't be for long. Just go and sit in the garden for ten minutes."

"What? The garden? It's practically winter!"

"Don't be ridiculous. It's barely autumn. Do what I ask for once," Helen snapped, losing her temper.

"Fine."

Tyler emerged from his room, too, barely glancing up from whatever game he was playing on his Switch handset.

She gave them a few seconds to get down the stairs and then darted into her son's bedroom and flung open a window to let some air in. As much as Reese drove her crazy, at least her bedroom didn't smell like a boy's changing room.

She checked there was nothing in the bedrooms that would show her up, straightened the beds out again, and then let herself breathe. She pasted on another fake smile, as though everything was just fine, and went back downstairs. She found the estate agents taking photographs and measurements of the kitchen.

"Everything all right?" she asked them. They were probably wondering what the hell had happened to her.

James smiled at her. "Yes, almost done down here and then we'll head upstairs."

"Great, thanks."

Helen moved out of the way to allow them both to traipse up the stairs. She hoped they weren't going to take long. She still had dinner to start, and she sensed the resentment coming from her children—who were still out in the garden—like actual shockwaves.

The thought of going through multiple viewings and offers, and people dropping out at the last minute, and house sales falling through depressed her.

She was stressed out and exhausted. The last thing she wanted to do was clean the bloody house all the time for viewings and argue with the kids to keep things tidy, but what choice did she have? Andy wasn't here most of the time so it wasn't as though he could do it.

She was excited for the move, though, in part because it would get her out of the crappy job she hated, answering customer service calls for an insurance company. At least Andy would be on a higher wage down there, so it would take the pressure off her having to earn. She still planned to work though. She couldn't be one of those women who had to ask their husbands for money.

She'd loved living in Bristol, but it was time for a change. The house they hoped to put an offer in on was right on the edge of Exeter and backed onto some gorgeous countryside. She pictured them all heading out for long family walks down the river. Not that they did such a thing here—in fact, she struggled just to get Reese out of her bedroom—but she could always dream.

The estate agents were being thorough, getting multiple photographs and taking measurements of each room. She appreciated they were doing a good job, but she did wish they would go already. She pictured Reese on the verge of blowing her lid outside and storming off, and she didn't have the emotional energy to deal with her teenager right now.

Finally, both men trotted back down the stairs.

"I don't think it's going to take long to sell," James Voysey said. "This is a perfect family home, well decorated, and a great layout. It being a new build means there's little maintenance to do, and it's energy efficient. Truly, it is a lovely home."

"Thank you," she said. "I'm sure you say that to all your clients."

"Oh, believe me, some of them would mean I was lying through my teeth."

She laughed and hoped he wasn't lying now.

He continued, "So the photos and details will be online within the next day or two, and the three-sixty virtual tour footage will take a little longer as it needs a bit more specialist work doing to it, but we've found it really does help people get a good idea if a house is for them without having to disturb you with actual viewings."

"That sounds good," she said with a relieved smile. "I can't stand time-wasters."

"Neither can we, and it really does help weed them out."

"Great." She showed them both to the door.

James shook her hand again, and Philip the photographer gave her a nod.

The two men left, and she was able to shut the door behind them. She remembered the children in the back garden and went to call them in.

"It's okay," she said, sticking her head out the back door to where both kids sat on the decking on the perfectly comfortable outside furniture. "They've gone. You can come back in now."

Reese shoved back the chair and stood. "Now we're not going to show you up, you mean?"

"Just come inside."

Reese glared at her as she pushed by. "I *hate* this."

Helen let out a sigh. "It's not exactly much fun for me either, sweetheart."

She glanced at the wall clock and counted down the hours until her husband would be home.

Chapter Four

Ryan called a briefing as soon as he got back in the office. It was already past knocking-off time, but with a case this big, everyone was going to be pulling some serious overtime.

He stopped by DCI Mandy Hirst's office to fill her in.

"I'd like to bring in extra hands for this one," he told her. "Four bodies are a lot for our team to handle."

She nodded in agreement. "As long as you can get the case solved, you can have as many people as you need. Got any theories so far?"

"Possibly the teenage son went off the rails and killed the rest of the family, but until we've had a report from SOCO and the post-mortems, we're just guessing."

"No witnesses?" she asked.

"None that we've found so far, though one of the neighbours heard something during the night. I've got a friend of the family who reported there being something wrong sitting in interview room one, and I'm hoping she'll be able to shed some light on the family situation. We've got uniformed officers doing interviews with the neighbours and we'll pick up from them if they find anyone who has seen or heard anything. It's a regular street with plenty of families living on it. Hopefully someone will have seen something."

"Yes, let's hope so. I'll see you in the briefing room."

"No problem."

Ryan left her office and crossed the floor to his desk. The place was a hive of activity, a constant thrum of background noise of phones ringing, people talking, and computer keys tapping. His desk was one place of calm, and that was how he liked to keep it. Everything was perfectly organised and in exactly the right place. If anything had been moved or misplaced, he found it impossible to concentrate until he'd set things right again.

He quickly printed off everything he needed for the briefing and took it to the briefing room. To a board on the wall, he pinned photographs of the crime scene, the bodies, names of the victims, and a local map with the location of the house pinned to it. As the case was gradually built over time, and they learned more about the family and made connections, the board would be added to. Some people liked to have everything online, but Ryan was still more old school. Computers were fine, but files could be easily missed. Just like how he preferred to take his notes using pen and paper, he liked to see things in real life.

As he worked, people filed into the room and took their seats. DCI Hirst was last to join them and positioned herself at the back of the room. From their time working together, he knew she'd allow Ryan to run things and would only step in if he needed her to.

Ryan took in the sight of his team—DCs Penn, Quinn, Kharral, and Dawson— and some new faces brought in for extra bodies. Mallory sat in the front row, her legs crossed, and a notepad balanced on her lap.

"Okay, everyone, thanks for coming." He ran through a roll call and then went over everything that had been learned so far.

"We believe the final person inside the house to remain alive was the sixteen-year-old son. He was found in his room with the murder weapon still embedded in his body. As of yet, we don't know if the stab wound was self-inflicted, but until we know one way or another, we treat the boy just like any of the other victims.

"I'm afraid we're all going to be working late tonight, but I'm sure you all understand why. We have four people dead, and time is of the essence. I'm going to need someone to coordinate with the uniformed officers to find out if there's anyone who needs to be interviewed in more detail. We already have one neighbour who believes they heard something around three a.m., so focus around that time. Someone else might have heard or even seen something and dismissed it."

"I can do that, boss," DC Linda Quinn offered.

He gave her a nod of thanks. She was good with the public and would be a calming influence on the shellshocked neighbours.

"I want any CCTV gone over. What street cameras do we have around the area? Check local shops and other businesses, and of course, find out if any of the houses on the street have home security cameras."

DC Craig Penn—the youngest member of their team—called out, "If the son was responsible for the murders, are we likely to see anything on street cameras?"

"Until we have proof that it was the son, we're keeping all our options open. I'm not going to let the bastard who did this get away because we were blindsided by chasing the wrong idea. For all we know, that's exactly what the killer wants us to do." Since Penn had been the one to single himself out, Ryan figured he might as well be the person for the job. "You can take the CCTV footage then, Craig. See what you can learn."

"Yes, boss."

"The house had a home alarm system," Ryan continued. He looked to DC Dev Kharral. "Dev, can you find out what company it was with and get the history on the alarm being disabled and armed. Also, find out what kind of information the company holds. Would anyone within the business have access to the security codes?"

Dev nodded and typed something into his phone.

"Shonda," he said, addressing DC Dawson. "Can you request their phone records. Each of the family members, including the eleven-year-old girl, had a mobile phone. I want their records, see if any calls were made during the night, or if there were any unusual call patterns showing in the days leading up to their murders."

"On it," she replied.

Ryan took in the other faces. "I want to find out everything there is to know about the lives of the Wyndhams. Who were their friends, what other family did they have? Where did they like to hang out, what are their hobbies? What about the kids' schools? How were they liked—especially the son? What were their jobs? Did they have any issues, drinking, gambling, drugs, things like that? They seem like a normal, middle-class family, but normal families don't end up slaughtered in their beds. There has to be a story behind this, and I want to know what it is."

Heads nodded in agreement.

"We also need to get a press report out. The newspapers are swarming like flies, and it's only going to get worse. A case like this will make national news." Ryan hardened his tone. "It goes without saying that I don't want anyone talking to the press. I'm sure they'll have a field day with the headlines about a murder house, but if I see so much as a whisper about our suspicions about the boy, I will come down hard on everyone."

He had to hope the neighbours wouldn't talk to the press too much and put any ideas in the reporters' heads. He didn't want a victim to be vilified in the press when there was currently little proof as to what had actually happened.

"I'm going to speak to the friend of the family who called this in, a Mrs Alison Perry. She's waiting in our interview room, and since she was close to the family, I'd like to hear what she has to say first hand. Does anyone have any questions?"

He gave them a minute to speak up, but it seemed they all understood what their actions were.

"Okay, thank you, everyone," he concluded. "Let's get to work."

Chapter Five

Ryan punched in the keycode for the interview room, waited for the buzz, and then pushed his way inside. An attractive red-haired woman in her late thirties sat on the opposite side of the room.

"Mrs Perry, I'm sorry to keep you waiting."

The woman glanced up at him with eyes rimmed with red, her skin blotchy and lips pale. She wrung a tissue between her hands. She closed her eyes briefly. "It doesn't matter. It's not like I'm planning to do anything else today."

"I am very sorry for your loss. Can I get you anything? A cup of tea? Coffee? Water?"

"No, I'm fine, really. I just want to get this over and done with."

"Of course." He could have done with a cup of coffee himself, but he didn't want to keep her waiting any longer than he already had.

"You understand that this is an informal chat and you're free to leave whenever you want," he told her. "I will be recording what's being said, but it's just standard procedure."

She didn't protest.

He pulled out the chair opposite to sit down, the chair legs screeching on the floor.

She tore another shred off the tissue and let it drop to the table. "I just want to help. I still can't believe someone would do this to them. They were good people."

"Because this doesn't look like a burglary, it really is vital that we learn everything we can about the family so we can start to build an idea about who might have wanted to do something so terrible."

"I'll tell you everything I can. I want you to find that sick son of a bitch as much as you do." She covered her mouth with both hands and inhaled as though she was suddenly fighting for breath. "Sorry."

"No, it's fine. I understand how traumatic this must be for you. Take your time, and if you need a break at any point, just say so."

"Okay, thanks."

"What's your relationship to the Wyndham family?"

"Just friends, but close friends. Our kids have grown up together." She closed her eyes briefly. "I have no idea how I'm going to break this news to my two. They're going to be heartbroken. They've gone from living in a world they've always seen as being safe to knowing something so...abhorrent can happen to innocent people." She gulped back another sob.

Ryan felt for her but needed to get her back on track.

"When was the last time you saw Liz Wyndham?"

She wiped her eyes. "At school on Friday. Because Dulcie hasn't been at the school for very long, Liz picks her up."

"Dulcie is eleven," he said. "She just started secondary school?"

"Yes, that's right, but Sheldon had only just finished. We met when the boys started primary school. We've all been friends ever since." Fresh tears filled her eyes.

"I'm sorry, I realise how hard this must be for you."

"I just can't believe someone would do this to them. They were a lovely family. How could someone hurt them like that?"

"That's what we're trying to find out." He checked the notes he'd written in his favourite stationery—an A5 Whitelines notebook. He had multiple duplicates of the notebooks in his drawer out of fear the manufacturer would stop producing them and then he'd be completely thrown. He always used a black Paper Mate InkJoy gel pen, too, and kept multiples of the exact same pen.

Alison suddenly straightened. "Oh God, have you told Conrad yet? He's going to be devastated."

Ryan frowned. He hadn't come across the name before. "Who is Conrad?"

Her eyes widened. "Conrad Smales is Sheldon's father. Hugh wasn't his real dad. He and Liz split up when Sheldon was only about three or four, I think. It was definitely before he started school, anyway. Liz met Hugh not long after, and they had Dulcie, that's why there's the big difference in age."

That was a vital piece of information they had missed. "We checked the surnames for each of the children and they were all under Wyndham?"

"Sheldon took his stepfather's name," she explained. "I don't think he wanted to feel as though he was different to the rest of the family, and Hugh had been in his life since he was only small."

Ryan wrote the name down. "That makes sense. I don't suppose you have any contact details for him?"

"No, I'm sorry, I don't, though I think he still lives in Bristol. We were friendly enough when the kids were small, but after he and Liz separated, I didn't really see that much of him. He had his son on the weekends like he was supposed to, but he didn't socialise with us after that."

"Not even with your husband?"

She shrugged. "You know what men can be like." She gave a small, tight laugh. "I mean, you are one. They never made the effort to see one another. My husband would want to go to the pub at the weekend, but then Conrad had Sheldon during those times, so things weren't as convenient as before."

This was information that couldn't wait until the end of the interview.

"Would you excuse me a moment, Mrs Perry?"

"Of course."

Ryan stepped out of the interview room and took out his mobile. He swiped the screen to bring up Mallory's name.

"Hey, I'm just outside," she said. "How's it going?"

"I need you to track down a Conrad Smales. I believe he lives locally."

"Who is he?"

"Sheldon Wyndham's real father."

"Shit. The teenager wasn't Hugh Wyndham's biological child then? How did we miss that?"

"Sheldon took the Wyndham name." Maybe Sheldon had always felt like an outsider in the family and so had taken on the name to feel like he was a part of things. Perhaps it hadn't worked? Was that enough of a motive to want his family dead?

A broken home? Perhaps resentment towards the stepfather and the mother for bringing a new man into their lives. Maybe hatred towards his half-sister for being the biological child of both parents? People had killed for less.

Ryan continued. "Check for any criminal history, particularly looking at any violence, possibly towards the son. Then I need you to track him down and then break the news to him about the death of his son and his ex-wife. You also need to bring him in for questioning and find out where he was last night."

"You think he might be a suspect?"

"Until it's proven otherwise, everyone is a suspect." He thought of something. "Hey, are you okay to work this late? I know time is getting on."

"Yeah, I'm fine. I've got my parents to come and stay over with Ollie. They understand it's a big case and I'm needed here."

"Will they be all right with him?"

"I'm sure they'll be fine. They can always call me if they need me."

Ollie had been suffering with night terrors since an accident at home, and Ryan had witnessed the effect it had been having on Mallory. They were used to not getting a huge amount of sleep in their job role, but with Ollie waking her almost nightly because of his bad dreams, the lack of sleep had been taking its toll on her.

"Okay. Let me know if anything comes up in his history and if you manage to track Smales down."

"Will do."

He ended the call and went back to the interview room. "Sorry about that."

Mrs Perry gave a small smile. "No, it's fine. He has a right to know."

Ryan took his seat once more. "Did Liz ever mention problems between her and her ex?"

"Just the usual stuff when people separate, complaints about him not doing enough or paying enough towards his son. I think things got easier after she'd met Hugh, and he picked up some of the slack."

"But there was no violence or anything like that?"

"No, not that I'm aware of."

Ryan jotted it down and then folded his hands on the table. "What about the relationship between Sheldon and his biological dad? How did they get on?"

"I don't think there was much of one recently, to be honest. Maybe they texted each other occasionally, but they didn't see much of each other. Conrad made the effort when Sheldon was younger, but Sheldon grew up, and I don't think he particularly wanted to spend much time hanging out with his dad."

"What about his stepdad? Did Sheldon get on with Hugh?"

She shrugged. "They fell out, of course. I mean, what parent doesn't fall out with a teenager from time to time. They like to push boundaries, don't they?"

"What did you make of Sheldon in general? I know teenagers can be difficult. How did he come across?"

"He was a sixteen-year-old boy. He could be moody, but can't they all at that age?"

"We noticed his room was full of heavy metal posters and horror films. Slasher flicks. Did he ever make you think that he was into things like that?"

"No more than any other teenage boy. My son's room looks exactly the same." Her eyes widened. "If you're thinking that Sheldon killed his family, let me tell you now that he wouldn't have done that. He just wouldn't, especially not to his sister."

"They weren't full siblings, though, were they? They had different dads?"

"Biologically, no, but they were as good as full siblings. They grew up together. I don't think he'd ever have hurt her or his mum."

He wasn't about to tell her that Sheldon had been the last one to be killed and that there was a chance he had his family's blood all over him. It was a convenient scapegoat for someone to make it look like an emo teen from a broken home had decided to take his anger and sadness out on his family, but then there was the alarm that hadn't been disabled and that there was no sign of a break-in to take into account.

She stared at him intently. "Really, whatever you're thinking about Sheldon, please stop it and focus on finding the real killer."

"We're just keeping our minds open to all possibilities, Mrs Perry. What about the relationship between Liz and Hugh? How did they get on?"

"Fine, as far as I'm aware. They're just a normal married couple. They had their disagreements, but nothing serious."

"Do you know if there were any issues like debt, or affairs, or alcohol or drug use? Maybe gambling problems?"

She jerked back, her mouth dropping open in surprise. "God, no. They weren't that kind of couple at all. I mean, they had a drink at the weekend and probably had a credit card or two, but certainly nothing that someone would murder the whole family over, if that's what you're implying."

"Again, just covering all bases." He glanced down at his notes. "I noticed there was an alarm system on the house. Do you know who might have access to the codes?"

"No one I can think of. I don't even have them. I assume the kids must have known it to get in and out of the house when they weren't home, but that's all."

"Do you think Sheldon might have given someone else the alarm codes?"

"It's certainly possible. You know what teenagers are like—they're not the most reliable of creatures. But he would have had it drummed into him that it needed to be kept a secret. Liz was quite paranoid about making sure it was set every time she went out and that no one saw her doing it."

He sat up, remembering that Sergeant Frome had mentioned that Liz Wyndham had put in a police report claiming that someone had been watching the house. "You describe her as being paranoid. Is that normal for her?"

She frowned as she thought. "Maybe a little, but I think she got worse recently. She was always worrying about strange things like a white van she didn't recognise being parked on the road or thinking one of the neighbours was spying on her. She didn't even want to have a home phone line because she said people could call it and if she didn't answer then they'd know she was out."

"Did something happen in particular that started the behaviour?"

She ran her hand over her face, appearing exhausted from the emotion and all the questions. Ryan felt bad that he was putting her through this after she'd just lost her friend, but it was important they know as much as possible.

"I...I'm really not sure. I just always took it as being who she was, but then this terrible thing has happened to her and her family." She looked up, meeting his eyes. "Do you think she was right to be paranoid? Do you think she somehow knew this was going to happen to her?"

"Honestly, it's still really early in the investigation so that's impossible for me to answer. At this point, we simply need to explore all the options. This white van you mentioned, did Liz ever describe it to you, or maybe mention if she saw who was driving or if there were any passengers?"

She shook her head. "Sorry, she just said a white van. I didn't ask for any more details."

"Is there anyone else she might have spoken to about her fears? Another friend, maybe?"

"Possibly, though I think I was always the person she was closest to. Her husband knew about it, but he used to get a bit irritated with the whole thing. I think he only agreed to the alarm system to try and keep her happy. Not that it did them much good." She suddenly thought of something and clapped both hands to her mouth. "Oh God, did you tell her mother yet? She lives up north and she's on her own. This is going to absolutely devastate her."

"I've got local officers in her area to go to her house to inform her about what's happened. Do you think she would have confided in her at all?"

"I doubt it. She wouldn't have wanted to worry her. She lives alone and she's so far away, it's not as though she could have done anything to help anyway. Losing her daughter and her grandchildren in such a horrific way is going to destroy her. How can anyone go on with their lives after a loss like that." Tears were streaming down her face now, and the piece of tissue was in tatters.

"You'd be surprised at what people can handle when they have to," he said, hoping it would bring her some comfort.

She sniffed and wiped her eyes. "I hope you're right. I just can't imagine never getting to see them again."

Ryan hoped he was right, too. He'd been in the position of having to deal with more than he thought his heart could ever handle. He might have survived it, but he hadn't been the same person since.

Chapter Six

It didn't take long for Mallory to find Mr Conrad Smales on the system. The unusual name helped her narrow it down, as did the Bristol address. He didn't have any kind of criminal record. With a little more digging, she brought up a mobile phone number attached to a social media profile and learned that he worked for a local haulage company.

She tried the mobile number first, but it went straight to answerphone. She gave it five minutes, in case he was on another call, and tried again. Still, the automatic answerphone cut in. It wasn't that she planned on giving him the terrible news about his son and ex-wife over the phone, but since he worked for a haulage company, she assumed there was a good chance he wouldn't be home.

When she didn't get any luck via the phone, she drove to his address. The flat was the ground one in a converted Victorian terrace, much like the one his ex-wife had owned, except hers had been the whole property.

She rang the bell and then knocked on the door.

No answer came, and she didn't get any impression of there being life on the other side of the door.

"Mr Smales?" she called out. "Police. I need to speak to you."

It was evening now, and most of the neighbours were home. She caught a woman in her fifties peeping out at her and motioned for to open the window.

"Can I help you?"

"Have you seen the man who lives here recently?" Mallory asked.

"No, sorry," she said and shut the window again.

Mallory sighed.

Still there was no answer. He must be out on a job. She hoped he wasn't going to hear the news from another source. No one should hear that their loved ones had died in such a horrific manner from a newspaper or social media post.

Unless, of course, there was another reason why she was unable to get hold of him and he'd made himself scarce because he knew of the family's death. Maybe he even had something to do with it.

Her next port of call would be the haulage company he worked for which was located in Cabot Park. She hoped they'd be able to tell her where Conrad Smales was right now.

Before she got back in the car, Mallory checked her phone to make sure she hadn't missed a call from her brother. Their parents were with him now, which eased her mind some, but she still worried. He'd woken up at three a.m. shouting, and she'd known he'd had his reoccurring dream about the fire. Something that might have only affected her a little had left a long-lasting mark on her brother's emotional well-being. He refused to use a toaster now, and was even nervous of the microwave, which meant they were down to him only being able to prepare himself cold sandwiches or cereal when he was home alone. She tried to convince herself that sandwiches and cereal were perfectly fine meals, but it hurt her heart that Ollie had gone backwards in his independence when he'd been doing so well.

Mallory was thirty-one now, and though she never would have admitted it out loud to anyone, a part of her was starting to wonder if she'd ever have a normal life of her own. Would she ever meet someone who would be willing to take Ollie on as well? She knew it would be a big ask, but she and Ollie came as a package deal, and she would never choose someone else over her brother. Despite knowing that, there was a tiny part that felt saddened by the idea, and maybe just the tiniest bit resentful. She wasn't a perfect person—she was just doing her best—but she hoped she didn't turn into a bitter old hag over it one day.

She drove the twenty minutes across the city to Cabot Park. At least at this time, the traffic was light, and she did the journey with ease. She assumed there would be someone still on the premises. Haulage companies worked twenty-four-seven.

Mallory pulled the car up outside. Several large trucks were parked on the forecourt, but there was no sign of any people. She climbed out and hugged her jacket tighter around her body. It was starting to get cold at night now. The air held the distinct salty, and slightly fishy tang of the estuary which was just on the other side of the industrial estate.

The office building was a grey single-storey portacabin. A yellow light glowed from behind the window, so she assumed someone was still working, though the office door was closed. She approached the building and tried to peer through the window, but the view was blocked by a set of dirty blinds. A number of dead flies balanced precariously on the slats.

Mallory stopped at the door and knocked. She was surprised when a deep male voice called out to her.

"Yeah?"

She tried the handle and cracked open the door, then reached to her pocket for her ID.

A man in his forties with a furrowed forehead and a pot belly that pressed into the edge of the desk he sat before deepened those furrows with a frown. "Help you?"

"I hope so. My name is DS Lawson, and I'm trying to track down one of your employees, Conrad Smales."

"What do you want with Conrad?"

"Police business, I'm afraid. He's not in trouble or anything, but I do need to find him. I assume he works here then?"

"Yes, has done for years. He's not working right now, though."

"When was his last shift?"

"He did a run yesterday and had today off."

"Where was his run to?"

The man frowned. "Hang on, let me check." He rifled through what appeared to be a logbook and then announced, "Newcastle."

"What time did he get back?" Mallory asked.

He looked at the book again. "Around oneish."

"In the morning," she checked.

"Yeah."

She'd thought if he'd been to Newcastle with work, it would be an automatic alibi for him, but if he got back at one in the morning, he might have still had time to kill the family. Unless he was with someone else, of course. He might have a girlfriend or a new wife who he went home to, so providing him with a different alibi. Until she tracked him down and found out for sure, she couldn't rule him out as being a suspect.

"I've been to his flat and tried his mobile, but I haven't been able to get hold of him. Do you have any idea where he might be?"

The man sniffed. "Sorry, I'm not the keeper of the people who work here. As long as they turn up for their shifts, they can do whatever they like outside of hours."

She gave a sweet smile that she didn't mean in the slightest. "I'm aware of that, I was just hoping there might be a pub or something that the people who work here hang out at."

He shrugged. "There's the Pig and Whistle down the road, towards Avonmouth. You might find him there."

"Can I check the phone number I have for him, in case I've been trying the wrong one?"

"I suppose. Give me a second to look it up."

He did, and she compared the two. It was the same number.

"Do you have a landline on file at all?"

"He never gave us one. Probably doesn't have one. Why bother these days when you can get by on a mobile. All a landline does is encourage spam calls."

He was probably right about that. She found more and more that people weren't bothering with a landline unless their internet provider insisted on having one. With how cheap mobile data was these days, it hardly seemed worth it.

"Thanks, I appreciate your help. Oh, before I leave you in peace, would you be able to let me have a copy of Conrad's shift pattern for the past week? That would be really helpful."

He eyed her with mistrust, so she widened the smile, feeling like her cheeks were about to crack. She tried to go with the idea that you caught more flies with honey than vinegar, though she was more than capable of dosing people with a good helping of vinegar, too, when the situation called for it.

"I suppose that would be all right," he grumbled.

She waited while he went on his computer and clicked through a couple of screens. A moment later, the printer in the corner hummed to life and spurted out a sheet of paper. The man rose to his feet and grabbed it off the printer and handed it to Mallory.

"There you go."

"Thank you, I appreciate your time. I didn't catch your name?"

"Peter," he said. "Peter Phipps."

"Thank you for your time, Mr Phipps."

He grunted again and dropped himself back into his seat. Mallory turned and left, grateful to be out of the stuffy little portacabin. She checked the address for the Pig and Whistle on her phone. He was right when he'd said it was down the road. It would only take her a matter of minutes to drive there.

Could Conrad Smales be dangerous?

The thought gave her reason to pause, and she used her phone again, but this time for a different reason.

"Hey, boss. I might have tracked Smales down to a pub at the end of St Andrews Road. Want to meet me outside before I go in?"

His voice came back down the line. "Absolutely. I'll be there in fifteen."

She'd feel better about having him there. As much as she wanted to be a strong independent woman who didn't take shit from anyone, she still had to be realistic, and going alone into a pub known for groups of truckers to hang out was one thing, but going into one as a police officer who was also trying to track down one of their own who might also have murdered his ex-partner's family was plain reckless.

She drove to the location of the pub and parked across the street. She did a bit of research on her phone on the haulage company until Ryan's car pulled up behind hers.

Mallory tucked her phone into the inside breast pocket of her jacket and climbed out of the car.

Ryan was already out of his and standing on the pavement. She instantly felt safer with him around. At well over six feet, his height was enough to make someone think twice before trying anything stupid. He glanced over at the front of the pub. A couple of large men stood outside the front, smoking.

"Good call on getting me to come along," he said. "This place looks dodgy as hell."

"I thought it was sensible, and since I haven't been able to get hold of Smales, and his work can't provide him with a solid alibi, I didn't want to rush into anything."

Ryan raised an eyebrow. "You think we might need to consider him as a suspect?"

"If he's made himself scarce straight after the family was murdered, then absolutely. He's got another shift at work tomorrow morning, and if he doesn't show up for that, we'll know for sure that something's not right. How did it go with the interview of the family friend? Did she have anything to say about him?"

"Not much. It had been some time since she'd seen him. She said there weren't any real issues between Smales and the Wyndhams, though, more that they were just distant."

"What about the son?" Mallory asked.

"She thinks there's no way he could be responsible. Says he's just a normal teenage boy."

She grimaced. "How well is a friend of the family really going to know a teenage boy? I'd say even the mother might not have known her son deep down."

Ryan shoved his hands into his trouser pockets. "You might be right. Shall we do this then?"

They crossed the street together, and Ryan led the way, pushing into the dingy innards of the pub. Mallory followed close behind. The pub wasn't busy, pockets of men gathered in murky corners. As Mallory had suspected, there was a noticeable lack of female clientele. The only woman was the one on her phone behind the bar.

"We're looking for a Mr Conrad Smales," Ryan said to the barmaid, showing her his ID.

She seemed bored. "Never heard of him."

Mallory swung her gaze around the room. "Do any of these men work at the lorry depot up the road?"

She jerked her chin towards one of the corners where four men sat around a table. "I think they do."

"Thanks for your help."

They approached the group of men who lifted their heads from their pints with expressions full of suspicion.

"Something we can do for you?" said the one closest.

Being the boss, Ryan took the lead. "We need to speak to one of your colleagues, Conrad Smales, and was told he might be found drinking here."

The man checked left and right as though searching for him. "He does normally drink here, but he's not been in today."

"Is that unusual, for him not to come in, I mean?"

The man shrugged. "Not really. I'm sure he's got other things going on in his life."

"Such as?"

"I dunno. I only work with the bloke."

Ryan's head turned towards the other men around the table. "What about the rest of you? Any idea where we might be able to find Conrad?"

"Is he in trouble with the law?" an older, weatherworn bloke said.

"Not at all. We have some news we need to deliver, and it really is vital we find him."

Mallory knew he was simply trying to ensure these men didn't feel the need to protect Conrad's whereabouts. Any hint that they wanted to talk to him about an entire family's murder might have them shutting down.

Weatherworn shrugged. "Sorry, mate. Can't help."

This was frustrating. They weren't getting anywhere, and she felt as though she'd wasted Ryan's time.

Ryan dropped his card on the table. "If he shows up, can you give me a ring?"

No one bothered to pick up the card.

"Sorry about that," Mallory said as they left the pub. "It was a wasted journey."

They came to a halt beside their cars.

Ryan took his keys from his jacket pocket and dangled them from a finger. "Not at all. I'd always rather you called me than you took a risk. Nothing worse than hearing about a colleague hurt while on the job and knowing it could have been prevented."

"You're right, thanks, boss." She let out a sigh. "Now what?"

"I'm going to circulate Smales' name as someone who needs to be chased, but you should go home. Not much more we can do for tonight. We'll have to see if Conrad shows up for work tomorrow and try and catch him there. You've got his schedule, right?"

"Yep, it's in my car."

"Good. Now go and get some sleep. I hope Ollie has a better night."

She offered him a grateful smile. "Thanks. See you tomorrow."

MALLORY FITTED HER key into the front door and opened it.

It had been a long day, and she was exhausted. Though she was looking forward to getting her head down, a knot of dread existed inside her. She knew there was little chance of her being able to sleep the whole night through. Ollie would most likely wake her at some point because of his night terrors. The experience had traumatised him, and the one place he'd always thought of as being safe—their home—now held the possibility of danger.

"Hi, I'm home," she called out.

She'd been expecting her parents' voices to answer, but instead it was a man's.

"In here."

She closed her eyes briefly and shook her head. Of course, it was Daniel's turn to sit with Ollie. She'd lost track of the days.

She went into the lounge where Ollie and Daniel sat over a large jigsaw puzzle. It was one of Ollie's favourite things to do, and she was glad for the hobby. Even though it took him weeks and even sometimes months to complete one, it kept him occupied and focused.

She mustered a smile for them both. "Hi. You look busy."

Ollie got up and came and gave her a big hug. "Hi, Mallory. Daniel's helping me. See, we're nearly done."

"Wow, well done you."

Ollie went back to his jigsaw.

Daniel Williamson worked for Helping Hands and came a couple of times a week to offer respite. He was laid-back and easy-going—the complete opposite of her. She could be hard and spiky, but she put that down as being a big sister who had to grow up defending her younger brother.

She'd got to know Daniel over the past few months, despite her not being there more of the time when he was around. Ollie chatted insistently about his new 'friend' and told her everything that Daniel had been doing—the football team he played for on a Friday night, the band he went to see, the takeaways he enjoyed—so even though she didn't spend much one-on-one time with Daniel, she still felt she knew him. She wondered how much Ollie told Daniel about her and hoped it was nothing embarrassing.

"How was work?" Daniel asked her. Then he saw her face and frowned, concern in his hazel eyes. "Is everything okay? You look tired."

She arched an eyebrow. "I assume that's not a compliment."

"Oh, no. I didn't mean it like that." He gestured towards her. "You look great. You always look great. Just tired, that's all."

She tucked her dyed black hair behind her ears and wished she'd thought to check her eye makeup in the rear-view mirror before she'd got out of the car. It was probably smudged halfway down her face, making her appear even more emo than normal. She was conscious that she probably didn't fit everyone's idea of what a detective looked like, and she'd done her best to tone down the style she'd cultivated in her twenties, but she had never been able to bring herself to get rid of it completely.

Ollie was staring at Daniel, trying to work out his reaction. "Daniel is embarrassed."

Mallory pressed a smile between her lips. It did seem that she had flustered him somewhat. "Yeah, well, work's really busy right now, and we haven't been sleeping too well, have we, Ollie?"

Ollie bent his head over his jigsaw. "Sorry, Mallory."

"It's okay, bud. It's not your fault."

Ollie's gaze darted towards Daniel. "I'm still having bad dreams."

Daniel twisted his lips. "About the fire?"

Ollie nodded.

Daniel patted him on the back of the hand. "I'm sure they'll stop soon." He got to his feet. "I'll be back in a couple of days, okay, Ollie? Do you think you'll have this jigsaw done by then?"

Ollie shrugged. "I don't know."

"I'll help again if you haven't, okay?"

"Okay." Ollie was already back engrossed in finding the next piece, so Daniel left him to it.

Mallory saw Daniel out, but he hesitated at the front door. "You know I didn't mean anything by it when I said that you looked tired. In my job, I see a lot of carers at breaking point, and it doesn't help the person they're taking care of if they do break."

"I'm not really a carer," she insisted. "It's not as though Ollie is sick or anything."

"No, but he does need you. You have a demanding job on top of taking care of Ollie, and I'm just wondering who is watching out for you."

"I'm a thirty-one-year-old detective. I'm perfectly capable of taking care of myself."

"You know I didn't mean anything by it. It's okay to be a strong person and still need help sometimes."

"I get help. You help, and so do our parents. It's just that no one is here in the night when things get bad."

"Can your parents stay overnight to give you a break, and maybe you go and stay at theirs?"

She shook her head. "As much as a full night's sleep sounds like heaven, I don't want to put that on them. Sometimes when Ollie has the nightmares, it's like he doesn't wake up properly and he's kind of trapped inside them. I don't think my folks are strong enough—physically or emotionally—to cope with that."

"There are other—"

She already knew what he was going to say and put up a hand to stop him. "No, I will not be considering any kind of care home for my brother. He's perfectly independent and was doing great before all of this happened. He'll get over it. It's just taking a bit of time."

"It wouldn't have to be forever. Just for a short time so you can get a break. It might even do Ollie some good to be out of this house. Like a reset for him. So he's not constantly thinking about the fire or worrying he might do it again. It might be the worry every day that's causing the nightmares. Maybe he needs to be somewhere he feels safe."

"He's safe here." She bristled. "He's safe with me. His confidence has taken a knock, that's all. I'm not going to palm him off on someone else just because of that."

"That's fine, I totally understand. You know Ollie better than anyone and will do what's best for him. Just don't forget that you're important, too."

He held her gaze for what felt like a fraction too long, and heat flooded her cheeks. She quickly glanced away. "I'd better get back to Ollie."

"Of course. Take care of yourself."

She nodded and, after he'd left, closed the door behind him.

What had all that been about?

Daniel was nothing like the sort of man she normally went for. She preferred a big build, tough kind of bloke, where Daniel was slight and fair and softly spoken. Not that any of her previous relationships had been anything to write home about, but then by the time the men found out she was not only a police officer, and normally panicked about whatever stupid shit they might have done when they were younger, but also learned about the important part Ollie played in her life, they tended to run for the hills. She was too serious for them, when all they wanted was a little fun, at least at the start.

"Mallory," *Ma-llor-wee,* "I need help."

She let out a tired sigh. "Coming, Ollie."

Chapter Seven

Ryan got into work the following morning.

Conrad Smales had been playing on his mind. Despite circulating his name, no progress had been made overnight in tracking him down. That the man had vanished not long after his son and his ex-wife's family had been brutally murdered didn't look good for him, despite there not being a motive they'd uncovered yet. Ryan hoped he had a good reason for going AWOL.

The moment Ryan's backside touched his chair, the phone on his desk rang.

"DI Chase," he answered.

"Morning, sir. It's Ben Glazier. I thought I'd let you know I've uploaded what we've processed from the crime scene so far, though I suspect we're going to be at the property for a few days to come. With the size of the house and the number of victims, it's going to take a while."

"I understand. Thanks for getting what you have to me."

"We've been working on it all night. I figured it was going to be information you'd need."

"You're right, it is. Anything specific of interest?"

"The blood on the clothes Sheldon Wyndham was wearing when he died *does* belong to the other members of his family. The pattern of the blood isn't what I would expect, though. It's been smeared as opposed to sprayed, which is what I'd have expected to see from the wounds on the other victims, especially those sustained by the mother."

"So, someone could have smeared the blood on him to make it appear as though he was the one responsible?" Ryan checked.

"That's how it looks to me. The murder weapon made for particularly interesting viewing. The only prints on both the handle and the blade were from Sheldon. If this was a knife he took from his own kitchen, I would have expected to find other family members' prints on there as well."

"He wiped it clean before he used it?"

"Possibly." Ben paused for a moment before continuing. "Also, the prints on the knife were from his right hand, which matches up as he was right-handed. They were positioned in an inverse hold, which is what I'd expect from someone who turned a knife on themselves, but something does bother me."

Ryan sat back. "Which is?

"I would have thought he'd use both hands at some point. It takes a lot of strength to stab yourself, and to drive a knife up into someone's skull. I'd be very surprised for him not to use both hands. Plus, the prints are very clean. Hardly any smudged or marked repeatedly onto the knife. It would have meant he'd kept his hand at almost the same position on the knife handle the entire time."

"Which is pretty unlikely."

"I'd say so."

Ryan processed what Ben had told him. Did that mean Sheldon Wyndham was innocent? He hoped he'd see Nikki Francis later that day and she could give him her thoughts as well. So far, it wasn't looking likely that the teen was the killer and more that someone had set him up, perhaps aware what conclusion they'd jump to. The school shootings in America had put boys like him in a bad light, and now a killer was trying to benefit from their assumptions. Good thing they had science to back them up.

"There's something else," Ben said down the line. "We found a couple of footprints in the blood upstairs. They're large and wide, and most likely belonging to a male, but it didn't match the sizes of either Sheldon or his step-father, Hugh."

"When you say footprints, do you mean shoeprints? Or actual footprints?"

"Actual footprints. Whoever they belonged to wasn't wearing shoes at the time. I'd say they weren't even wearing socks."

Ryan frowned, mulling that over. Who gained access to another person's house and removed their shoes and socks before killing everyone there? Maybe they were trying to be quiet and thought not wearing shoes would help that?

"What about DNA from the footprint?" Ryan asked. "Have you been able to get anything from it?"

"With combined samples, such as with blood, we need a sample to be at least twenty percent of the whole. I'm afraid with the amount of blood that was on the floor, there isn't much chance of us getting a good enough sample from the print to be of any use."

"Damn it."

"Sorry," Ben apologised, though it wasn't his fault.

Something else bothered Ryan. "Why wasn't there any blood found downstairs? If the perpetrator left the house after the murders, surely he would have tracked at least some of the blood down the stairs."

"Could the killer have left from an upstairs window?"

"They were all locked from the inside. The only way out was through the front or back door."

"Both of which had been locked as well," he said.

"Whoever did this had everything meticulously planned. I think the killer took time to clean himself down, maybe even changed his or her clothes. They'd have been covered in blood unless they'd taken the time to wash and change." He was thinking out loud now. "What condition was the bathroom in? Was there blood on the floor?"

"Yes, blood was found in there. The killer might have gone via the bathroom to wash off their hands—maybe there was too much blood on the knife, and it was making it too slippery to grip."

Ryan sucked air in over his teeth. "I think it was more than that. Whoever killed this family would have been covered in blood, including in their hair, so there's a chance they washed it out. They used the place to clean down before leaving the house."

It was almost as if the killer had treated the house like his own.

"My officers are paying extra attention to gathering DNA and prints from the bathroom. If the killer was wearing protective gear and took it off in the bathroom, they might have shed hairs or clothing fibres. We'll check the plughole and pipes for hairs as well." Ben continued, "Fibres were also found that haven't been matched to anything else in the house."

"What kind of fibres?"

"Sheep's wool."

"From a jumper, maybe?"

"Possibly. Also, we found hemp fibres."

Ryan straightened in his seat. "Hemp, like marijuana? Maybe from the boy's room, if he was a smoker."

"No, these fibres are different. More like the kind you'd find that had been turned into clothing or material for a rope."

"Rope? There weren't any obvious signs that the victims had been tied up."

Maybe Nikki would find signs that they had been during the post-mortems. More fibres on the victim's skin, perhaps. The initial view of the scene had looked as though the killer had disturbed the victims in bed and used a chair under the door to keep the younger members of the family trapped in their rooms, but perhaps that, too, had been a setup, like making it seem as though Sheldon had been the one responsible.

Something else occurred to Ryan. Why hadn't the two children tried to get out of their windows upon finding their doors jammed? Had they not thought of it? Or had there been another reason?

He made a mental note to go back to the house and take a second look.

Another thing confused him. If the children had woken up and heard their parents' murders and tried to get out of the room, wouldn't one of the neighbours have heard them shouting? Either the killer moved fast and almost silently, and the kids didn't wake up, or something else had happened.

"That's about it," Ben finished off. "I've uploaded the report which has everything in more detail, and if you have any questions about the findings, you've got my number."

"Absolutely. Thanks, Ben."

"Not a problem. Hope you catch whoever did this."

"So do I."

He ended the call. Everyone was back in the office for the day now, so he called a quick briefing for that morning to make sure everyone knew what they needed to be doing for the day.

Ryan stood in front of his team.

"We got the forensic report back," he told them. "The blood found on the boy's body did belong to his mother, sister, and stepfather, but there's a possibility someone else smeared it onto him to make it appear as though he committed the murders and then killed himself." He went through the information about the fingerprints and the footprint in the blood. "Right now, I think we're looking for someone outside of the home." He focused on Mallory. "Any luck on tracking down the biological father yet?"

"No, sorry. I swung by the flat on my way in, but there still wasn't any answer, and the neighbours said they hadn't seen him. He's still not picking up his phone."

"Okay, thanks. We need to make it a priority today that we locate him. If he doesn't show up for work today, let's get a warrant to ping his phone location."

She nodded. "Agreed. He should be back in work this morning, so I'll check again there. If he doesn't show up, we're going to have to assume he had something to do with the murders."

Ryan turned his attention to DC Quinn. "Linda, how did you get on with the neighbours?"

"We have a second neighbour, Mrs Stephanie Rice at number forty-three, who says she thought she heard a thud come from the house shortly after three."

"Thought she heard?" If what the neighbour had heard was Liz Wyndham falling out of bed while trying to escape, it helped to corroborate the time the murders occurred and would help them to narrow down any searches on CCTV.

"She said she was half asleep and so couldn't be certain she hadn't dreamt it. The only reason she thought to notice the time was that she'd woken up late the previous day and didn't want to oversleep again."

"What about any of the other neighbours? Did they see or hear anything around the same time?"

Linda shook her head. "Not that we've found so far. Everyone else claims they slept peacefully all night."

Ryan did his best not to roll his eyes. "Typical that it happens on a street where apparently no one suffers from insomnia. Four people in a house, and yet no one woke up and tried to get help? Why were they all sleeping so soundly? We're also assuming the killer took the family's mobile phones and placed them in the freezer while they were asleep. They must have entered each room and located the phone with no one waking up. If they weren't wearing any shoes, that would have made them quieter, but it still doesn't quite add up to me."

"Does this mean we're ruling Sheldon Wyndham out of the running?" DC Craig Penn asked.

"Not completely. I want to find out what the post-mortems reveal before we come to any conclusions. Let's keep our minds open."

Mallory put up her hand. "Sheldon could have had an accomplice. Maybe he was the one who let the killer into the house."

"That's a possibility, too. Or one of the other family members did, and things didn't go to plan. We're still digging into the lives of Liz and Hugh Wyndham. Maybe they have skeletons in the closet. Perhaps one of them was supposed to survive?" Ryan looked to Craig. "How far have you got with the CCTV?"

Craig checked his phone for notes. "One of the houses about ten doors away had security cameras. I've been through the footage from that night, but so far I haven't spotted anything on it that would help."

"What about the cars parked in the street?"

"They're all associated with the people who live there. Nothing strange to be accounted for. I've requested footage from a couple of nearby shops as well, so that might give us something."

"Okay, keep trying."

Dev Kharral spoke up. "Boss, I've heard back from the security company that the family got their alarm system from. They've emailed me a report on that system going back to when they first had the alarm installed, and it's definitely interesting."

"In what way?"

"Up until a few weeks ago, the alarm was set and disabled a couple of times a day, mainly first thing in the morning, when I assume the family was leaving for work and school, and then it was disabled again around four p.m. when they were all coming back home, and then it would be set again around eleven p.m."

Ryan nodded. "That all sounds normal. What changed?"

"Everything. The usual pattern went out the window, and the alarm started to be set and disabled during random times of the day *and* night."

"Didn't the family notice the change?"

"Not that they reported. The panel that shows the history is only small and part of the keypad, and you have to select the correct setting to show the history, so unless they had a reason to check it, they wouldn't have seen it automatically." He got to his feet and handed Ryan a printout. "I've done a comparison of the two different times and highlighted the ones that didn't fit in with the previous pattern."

"Good work."

Ryan bent his head over the paper and studied the findings. Where the initial couple of weeks were regular, as DC Kharral had said, the extra entries didn't seem to have any pattern at all. Some were in the daytime, other times during the middle of the night. On some occasions the alarm was disabled and reset within twenty minutes of each other, and, on others, hours passed between the two settings.

"This means one of two things," Ryan said. "There was a glitch with the alarm, or someone was manually resetting it. The question is, was the person resetting it someone inside the home or outside?"

"It could have been the boy sneaking in and out of the house at night?" Kharral suggested.

Ryan nodded. "That sounds feasible. Or perhaps he was sneaking someone in, maybe a girlfriend, or even a boyfriend? How much have we learned about him so far?"

"Honestly, not a huge amount," one of the DCs from outside of his team said. "We spoke to his teachers at school, who said he was a bit of a loner. He wasn't the kind to take part in any clubs, and no one mentioned any girlfriend at all. I didn't get the impression he was some kind of rebel who sneaks out at night, or who sneaks his girlfriend in."

"Okay, thanks. How are we getting on with the family's phones?

Shonda Dawson spoke up. "We've had the reports back on the family's devices."

"Anything of interest showing up, particularly on Sheldon's phone?"

She shook her head. "Not on the boy's, but there is something on the father's phone."

Ryan laced his fingers in front of his body. "Tell me."

"There weren't any recent anomalies, but several months ago multiple calls were made and received from the same number to Hugh Wyndham's phone."

"Do we know who the other number belongs to?"

"It's not registered, unfortunately, but we're still looking into it."

Ryan thought for a moment. "Let me know as soon as you know who that number belongs to."

"Will do, boss."

"It's far more likely that whoever did this knew the family. That's going to be our key to pinning this down, I'm sure of it." He surveyed their faces. "Let's make the next twenty-four hours count."

Chapter Eight

The last thing Mallory had been expecting was a call from the sullen man at the lorry depot.

"Thought you'd want to know that Conrad's here," Peter Phipps told her. "He showed up for work as normal."

Mallory was instantly on her feet, grabbing her car keys. "Hold on to him for me. Don't let him leave."

"How am I supposed to do that? He's got a job to do."

She spoke with the phone clamped to her ear. "Tell him there's something wrong with his lorry. I'll be there as soon as I can."

Irritation made him snappy. "I'm trying to run a business here."

"And I'm trying to do my job, too. Please, it's important. He needs to know what we have to tell him. I'm literally minutes away."

She ended the call and looked around the office. Ryan was nowhere to be seen, but she wasn't going to go and bring Conrad Smales in on her own. Craig was sitting at his desk, looking bored as he went through CCTV footage.

"Hey, Craig, you fancy a drive. I've found Smales."

"Absolutely, Sarge." He put his computer to sleep and got to his feet, picking up his jacket from the back of his chair.

"Great. I'll drive."

They hurried out to her car. Mallory drove as fast as she dared to the lorry depot, hoping Conrad hadn't left already. If he had, she'd have to get the lorry's licence plate number circulated as an attention drawn and get the highways agency to stop it on the motorway and then bring him in. She was sure they could all do without the drama.

They arrived at the depot and she and Craig headed straight for the portacabin. Peter Phipps saw them come in and he lifted his chin to where a man was sitting by the water cooler, his head in his hands. She flashed Phipps a grateful smile.

"Mr Smales." She held up her ID. "I'm DS Lawson and this is DC Penn. Can we have a chat?"

Conrad Smales looked up. He was a jowly man in his fifties with a spiderweb of capillaries across his nose and cheeks. He seemed to be a fair few years older than Liz Wyndham had been, and Mallory wondered if that had been the reason they'd broken up all those years ago.

He frowned at her. "I'm supposed to be out on a delivery."

"I'm sorry, but this really is more important. I'm afraid it would probably be better if we go down to the station. I do have some questions I need to ask you."

He scowled and gestured to the window and the huge vehicles outside. "I have to work."

Mallory shook her head. "Not today you don't."

She didn't want to tell him about his son and ex-wife while they were here.

"It's fine." Phipps grunted. "I'll get your run covered."

Conrad unfurled and rose to his feet, revealing well over six feet of body and a decent-sized gut. "Are you going to tell me what this is all about at least?"

Mallory hesitated and then said, "I'm afraid it's about your son."

"Sheldon? What's he done?"

She was surprised Conrad hadn't already heard about the murder. It had been all over the news.

"He hasn't done anything, but I do really need to talk to you about him."

That seemed to placate Conrad enough, and they left the portacabin together.

"Can you put your hands on the roof of the car," Craig said.

"Why?"

"Just routine."

Conrad did as he was told and Craig patted him down for any possible weapons. "All clear." Craig opened the back door and Conrad climbed in. Mallory got behind the wheel.

They sat in silence as she drove them back to the station. She found her usual parking spot. "Thanks, Craig," she told the DC. "I'll take it from here."

"No problem, Sarge."

She showed Conrad through the building to one of the interview rooms.

Mallory gestured for him to take a seat. "Can I get you anything? Coffee? Tea?"

"No, all I want is for you to tell me what the fuck is going on?"

He was still standing beside the table.

"Please," she said, "sit down, Mr Smales."

He appeared to be thinking as though he was going to give her an argument about it, but then must have realised that the quickest way to get what he wanted was to do as she asked, and he sank into the seat.

Mallory took the chair on the opposite side of the table. "I'm afraid I have some terrible news about Sheldon, and your ex-wife, Liz, and the rest of her family."

His eyes widened. "What's happened?"

"They were killed in the early hours of Monday morning."

"What? Killed how? In an accident?"

"We're currently treating this as a murder investigation."

His jaw dropped. "They were murdered." He clamped his hand over his mouth. "My God. You're telling me Sheldon and Liz are dead?"

"I'm very sorry. Hugh and Dulcie were also killed."

"Jesus Christ, you're making it sound like they were slaughtered."

"I'm sorry," she said again.

His face drained of colour. "Do you know who did it?"

"It's something we're still looking into. I am going to need to ask you some questions about your whereabouts when the murders happened."

He shook his head. "You can't think I had anything to do with it?"

"It's simply a formality. I would like to record our conversation, however, and I do need to tell you that you do not have to say anything. But it may harm your defence if you do not mention when questioned something which you later rely on in court. Anything you do say may be given in evidence."

"What is this? Am I under arrest?"

"Not at all, Mr Smales. You're free to go at any time. But considering what's happened, I'd like to think you'd want to do everything you can to help us find whoever did this to your son and ex-wife's family. Unless you have a reason not to."

"No, of course I don't," he spluttered.

"Good then, we're on the same page. You haven't been an easy man to track down. Where have you been for the past twenty-four hours, Mr Smales?"

"I'm a lorry driver. I did a delivery to Newcastle yesterday. I left at eight a.m., drove eight hours, what with traffic and a couple of stops, and then had to wait for the lorry to be unloaded, which took several hours, and then drove back again. I didn't get back until the early hours, and then I turned off my phone so I could sleep."

"You're saying you've been at home, but your phone was switched off?"

"That's right."

"I went to your flat yesterday, Mr Smales, and banged on the door. Why didn't you answer?"

He shrugged. "I obviously didn't hear you. It's hard to sleep when you're working strange hours, so I tend to put in ear plugs."

She struggled to hide her disbelief. "You wore ear plugs all day and had your phone switched off?"

"There's no law against turning off your phone. I don't always want people to be able to get in touch with me, night and day."

Even your own son? she didn't say.

"If we were to check with your phone company, we'd see a pattern of that behaviour? It's not unusual for you to switch it off?"

"No, it isn't."

Mallory jotted a note down to make sure she remembered to do just that. She folded her hands on the table. "Do you live alone, Mr Smales? Is there anyone who can attest to your whereabouts?"

"No, there isn't. It's just me."

"When was the last time you saw or spoke to your ex-wife or your son?"

He frowned slightly as he thought. "I last saw Sheldon couple of weeks ago, I suppose. I couldn't tell you when I last saw Liz, but it's been months."

"That seems like a long time."

"I've been busy. Please don't judge. Sheldon is almost an adult." Conrad caught himself, and his gaze flicked away. "I mean, he *was* almost an adult. He wasn't interested in spending time with his dad anymore."

"How did you get on with your son?" she asked.

"We probably weren't as close as I would have liked." He swiped tears from his eyes. "Something I'm going to regret for the rest of my life."

"How would you describe your breakup with Liz?"

His lips thinned with displeasure. "It was a long time ago."

"Was it her decision or yours?"

"More hers, if I'm honest. I was pretty broken up about it at the time. She wanted a trial separation, and then she met someone else and that was that."

"Someone else who took over your family? I imagine that would leave you feeling very bitter?"

His head shot up. "Not bitter enough to murder my ex-wife's family and my own son, if that's what you're implying. Besides, it was almost thirteen years ago. Don't you think, if I'd felt that way, I'd have snapped a lot sooner?"

Mallory watched his body language and tone. Did he have a short temper? Was his defensiveness what she'd expect or was he hiding something? "People can hold onto grudges for a very long time, Mr Smales. I notice you've never remarried, never gone on to have another family yourself."

His jaw tightened, and he glanced away once more. "No, I wasn't going to put myself through that again. I was better off on my own. Only have myself to rely on or worry about."

She got the feeling he still harboured a lot of pain and resentment about his marriage breaking down. "You didn't worry about your son at all?"

"He was in good hands," he paused, "or so I thought."

Mallory switched tactics slightly. "Did Sheldon ever give you any hint that he was a violent person?"

Conrad met her eye. "You mean because of all the black clothing and the heavy metal? You don't think Sheldon could have hurt them?"

She offered him a sympathetic smile. "We're just covering all bases right now. Could he have got involved with someone who might have wanted to hurt them? Maybe he mentioned someone he met online?"

"I have no idea what he did online. What are you suggesting? That Sheldon met some deviant on the internet, and he let them into the house so they could come in and slaughter him and his entire family?"

"We need to remain open to all possibilities. Our digital forensics teams have taken all phones and laptops from the house and are working through them. If there's anything incriminating on them for us to find, then we will find it."

"Good." He bunched his fists. "I want you to find out who did this. I promise you, Detective, I didn't have any involvement whatsoever."

She wasn't sure whether to believe him or not.

"Oh, one more question, Mr Smales. Do you have the codes to the alarm system or keys for the house?"

"No, of course not. It's not my home."

"Can you think of anyone who might have had them?"

"You're asking the wrong person. I really wasn't close enough to the family to know."

She raised an eyebrow. "You weren't close to your son's family?"

"Like I said, that's something I'm going to live to regret. When can I see Sheldon? I want to see him one last time."

"There will be an autopsy due to the way he died, but I can arrange for you to visit his body soon."

He nodded. "Yes, I want to say goodbye."

She gave him a sad smile. "I understand."

"What about a funeral? When will I be able to get him back?"

"Not for a while, Mr Smales, I'm sorry. I'll have a Family Liaison Officer get in touch with you and they'll be able to explain what to expect."

Mallory thought she'd covered everything. "Thank you for your time, Mr Smales, and I truly am sorry for your loss." She slid her business card across the table towards him. "There may be some further things that come up during the investigation that we'll need to talk to you about, so I would like to request that you make yourself available to us—no more turning off your phone—and if you think of anything that may help, please do call."

He nodded and took the card.

Chapter Nine

Ryan glanced up from his desk to find Mallory approaching.

"How did it go with Smales?" he asked her. "Did he give any explanation why we weren't able to contact him over the past twenty-four hours?"

"It went well. He says he sleeps strange patterns due to his working hours and that's why he was out of contact. I've got some things I need to follow up on, mainly contacting his mobile provider and making sure their records fit his story of him regularly switching his phone off for lengths of time to sleep."

"Did he have an alibi?"

"No, he was home alone, and he didn't finish his job until one a.m. the morning of the murders."

Ryan pursed his lips. "But could he have had time to kill them all?"

Mallory nodded. "If he was at the depot at one a.m., that still would have given him time to murder the family and get home. If his phone was conveniently off, there's no way of proving he was home all that time as we wouldn't be able to trace it."

"What about motive?"

"I'm not sure. He seemed to have a lot of built-up pain and resentment about his marriage breaking down, even thirteen years later. Liz met Hugh, and so Conrad was a jilted husband. Then there's Sheldon to consider. Conrad says they didn't see much of each other now that Sheldon was older, so perhaps he felt that as another rejection? Maybe that was enough."

He exhaled a breath and shook his head. "I don't know. It's been a long time since they broke up. Why wait until now?"

"Maybe the son not wanting to see him made things worse? There could have been arguments that we're not aware of, I mean, it's not as though we can interview the victims."

"No, but we have their phones and their laptops. We might find something on there, emails or text messages. If the phone records show him calling any of the family members more than normal, it could indicate there was more going on than he's let on."

Ryan's phone rang, and he held up a finger to Mallory to tell her to give him one minute.

He answered the call, "DI Chase."

"Ryan, it's Nikki. I thought you'd want to know that we're finished with the post-mortems on the victims."

"That was fast."

"I brought in a couple of extra pathologists. It's a big case, and I know time is of the essence. You want me to run through the findings?"

Ryan was already on his feet. "I'll come to you. See you shortly."

He ended the call and turned to Mallory who was still standing beside his desk. "You want to come and get the post-mortem reports with me?"

She nodded. "Absolutely. Let's hope they can shed some light on what really happened."

THIRTY MINUTES LATER, Ryan pulled up into the car park of the single-storey building, and both he and Mallory climbed out. The public mortuary was located just outside Bristol and had been purpose-built.

Nikki was waiting for them at reception. "Come on down. I think you'll find this interesting."

"Any chance the killer left his business card embedded in one of the bodies," Ryan only half joked.

She smiled. "Nothing quite as convenient as that, but eye-opening just the same."

She led them down the corridor, and they all donned protective outerwear and entered the autopsy room.

Four stainless-steel tables were positioned at equal spaces across the room. On top of them, beneath sheets, lay the bodies of the family—one noticeably smaller than the others.

Nikki Francis wasn't the only pathologist in the room. An older man, Brian Stewart, was also assisting, though the others must have moved onto other cases. With this many bodies to get through, and with time being of the essence for them to unravel exactly what had happened in that house, it was important they have all hands on deck.

Both Ryan and Mallory nodded a greeting to him as they entered.

"Where do you want to start?" Nikki asked.

"Let's start with Sheldon Wyndham. I feel like he holds more of a key to what happened than the others." Ryan didn't know exactly which bodies were beneath which sheets, but he could take a good guess from the sizes of the shapes underneath them.

Nikki nodded. "Very well." She approached the third table and pulled back the sheet to reveal the teenager's body beneath. "Sixteen-year-old Sheldon Wyndham, five feet eleven inches, one hundred and eighty-one pounds. The fatal injury is a vertically placed knife wound to the abdomen which perforated the abdominal aorta. He would have died within minutes."

Was that a lucky strike to have hit the aorta or did whoever stab Sheldon have some kind of anatomical knowledge? There was one big question Ryan needed answering. "Did he stab himself, or did someone else do it?"

"Vertical knife wounds tend to imply murder, where horizontal wounds are more likely to be self-inflicted. The track of the knife wound is upwards and backwards which also tends to indicate murder. If you were going to stab yourself in the stomach, how would you do it?"

Ryan thought for a moment, picturing a large kitchen knife in his hand. It had a weight to it—not heavy by any means, but solid. Mentally, he turned it inwards and pictured the point of the blade aimed for his guts.

"I'd hold it in both hands," he said. "One behind the other. I'd want to go fast and deep, so I'd want as much power behind the knife as possible."

"So, the blade would be straight or possibly slightly downwards?"

"Yes. I suppose so." Holding the knife in both hands at an upwards angle would put his shoulders and biceps into an awkward position.

"The way this knife has been driven into the body looks to me as though it's come from an upwards strike." She mimicked the motion of someone bringing a knife underarm rather than over and down. "The other thing that caught my attention is how deep the wound is. What do you think the natural thing to do is when you're stabbing yourself?"

Ryan shook his head. "I'm not sure."

"You'd pull back. Even if you wanted to die, the body's natural reflexes are to avoid pain, and so even if you knew what you were doing, it would be hard not to."

"Hard, but not impossible?"

"No, not impossible, but this knife wound is deep—almost to the victim's spine. It would have taken not only considerable force, but also some steely determination to keep going that deep."

Ryan remembered what they'd learned from the prints on the knife, how it had only been the prints from Sheldon's right hand. Could he have stabbed himself with that much force with only one hand? It seemed unlikely.

"I also checked the victim for any scars or cuts that might indicate previous self-harm and found none. Someone who was considering suicide would most likely have self-harmed at some point, but there's no evidence of that here."

"What about the blood found on the body?" Ryan asked.

"I can say that the blood found on his body does match each of his family members, but the blood spatter is all wrong. If you check photographs taken at the crime scene, the blood spatter of the mother when her throat was cut went in an arc. There's no way he could have avoided that if he was leaning over her with the knife."

"That's the same conclusion forensics came to with the clothes," Ryan said. He turned to Mallory. "So far it seems far more likely that someone has tried to make it appear as though he killed his family rather than him actually being the one responsible for the deaths."

Mallory nodded. "I agree. Someone has done a bad job of trying to cover their own tracks."

This job would have been far easier if it had been the boy who'd killed the family. An open-shut case of a teen who, in a mental health crisis, decided to take out his anger on those closest to him. Now they had a killer out on the streets who'd somehow got in and out of a locked, and alarmed house, and had planned the attack enough to fool the police, at least initially.

"There's something else," Nikki said. "Something came up in the tox screen that I think you'll find of interest."

"What?"

"All four of the victims had traces of diphenhydramine in their systems. It was in the boy's system as well, which also helps to build the case for him being a victim and not the perpetrator."

"Diphenhydramine," he repeated. He knew that name.

Mallory filled it in for him. "Sleeping pills. It's the drug most commonly used in over-the-counter sleeping medications."

Nikki smiled approvingly. "That's right."

Ryan frowned. "Someone didn't want them to wake up. It explains why someone was able to move around the house and take their phones, and why they didn't wake up quickly enough to raise the alarm when the attack started."

"But for that to have worked," Mallory said, "they'd have needed to be drugged earlier that evening."

Ryan agreed. "Someone must have had access to the family's food for them to have slipped them something. We need to find out exactly what they ate and drank that evening. Did they go out to eat, or did they order a takeaway, or cook at home?"

Nikki took a couple of steps around the table. "I can help with that. They all had the remains of some kind of beef stew in their stomachs when they died."

Beef stew wasn't the sort of thing people normally ordered for a takeaway.

Ryan thought for a moment. "If they cooked at home, and didn't bring anything in from the outside, we might be looking at someone who was able to gain entry to the home. Just because it wasn't the boy doesn't mean it wasn't someone they knew. Maybe they even had dinner with that person the evening before they died."

"Like the boy's father," Mallory suggested.

Ryan shook his head. "He drove his lorry to Newcastle that evening. He wasn't in Bristol. He couldn't have slipped anything to them."

"Unless he'd already done it," she said. "If the killer knew their habits, perhaps he could have pre-planned what they were going to eat or drink and then laced whatever that food or drink was with drugs. If it was enough to make the victims sleep so deeply that they wouldn't hear the alarm being disabled or reset and allow the killer to make their way through the house without being disturbed."

Ryan blew out a breath. "That would have taken some planning, but I guess it's possible."

"So, this person was creeping around their house while the family was drugged and sleeping," Mallory said, "moving their things around, jamming chairs under door handles, and basically getting the house ready for them to all be slaughtered, all while they slept."

Ryan was starting to build up a mental image of the killer. Cold, calculated, a forward planner, someone who wasn't easily spooked. Could it really have been Conrad Smales? He hadn't met the man himself, but perhaps that needed to change.

"We're going to need SOCO to go through every consumable item in the kitchen and find out if any of it has been laced with diphenhydramine."

"They might have disposed of it when they left the house," Mallory said.

"Yes, but it's still worth checking."

Ryan remembered they still had three more family members.

"What about the others?" he asked Nikki. "Anything that might help us find out who did this?"

"Because the father was killed so quickly, he didn't have time to fight back. His nails were dirty, but there was no DNA belonging to anyone else underneath them. The mother has some bruising on her knuckles where she may have put up a fight, but her nails were completely clean, as were her hands, and so I'd say the killer cleaned them after she was dead to remove any DNA. The girl didn't fight back as far as I can tell."

Ryan closed his eyes briefly against the image of the girl being too frightened to defend herself. "I wonder if that's because she knew her killer."

"Possibly, or she might have just frozen. It's common for people to do that in times of intense fear."

Had the poor girl been aware of her parents being murdered at that point?

They finished up going over the findings and left the examination room, stripping off their outer protective wear and dumping it in the hamper outside. They paused in the corridor.

Mallory seemed to sense there was friction between Ryan and Nikki. "I'll meet you back at the car."

Ryan nodded. "Won't be a sec."

Ryan and Nikki fell silent as Mallory left and then faced each other.

"I'll send everything through as well," Nikki said, "but if you have any questions, you can always call." She paused and then added with a smile, "assuming you still have my number."

"Yes, I'm sure I do."

Ryan knew she was just teasing him, but it still made him feel like he'd acted like a prick towards her.

"And keep me updated," she said. "I'd like to know how this pans out."

"I will."

She looked as though she was going to walk away for a moment, but then she turned back to him. "You can get in touch for reasons outside of work, too, Ryan. If you want."

"I'd like that...it's just work...it's crazy busy right now."

She arched her brow. "You don't have to make excuses. I'm a big girl. I can take it."

"Would you believe the old 'it's not you, it's me' line?" he offered.

She looked him up and down. "Actually, yes, I would."

He gave a small chuckle. "Well, good, because it is."

"I'll see you, Ryan," she said and spun on her heel and walked down the corridor, away from him.

Ryan sighed and went to join Mallory at the car. He checked his watch. Time was getting on.

"You mind if I drop you back at the station?" he asked Mallory.

"Of course not."

He had somewhere he needed to be.

Chapter Ten

After he'd dropped Mallory back, Ryan drove to the hospital.

He found his way to the oncology ward with ease. This wasn't his first time here.

He recognised one of the nurses on the reception desk, nodded his hello, and continued through to the day room where several people sat in high-backed chairs and were positioned around the outside of the room. It took him a moment to pick his ex-wife out of the patients. He still hadn't got used to seeing her without any hair. It'd always been a source of pride for her when they'd been married, and she rarely missed an appointment with the hairdresser, but now those locks were no more. She hadn't wanted to go down the wig route, claiming that she didn't feel any need to hide what was wrong with her, and he respected her for that.

It was strange how the people she shared the room with were all so different—young, old, male, female, thin or fat—and yet all somehow shared that similar appearance.

Donna had been sitting with her eyes closed, her head rested against the back of the chair, but she must have sensed someone entering and she sat up and caught his eye. She gave him a tired smile and lifted her hand in a half wave.

Ryan returned the smile, reminded of the old adage to fake it till you make it, and walked over.

"How are you feeling?"

She shrugged. "Tired, as usual. You didn't have to come. I could have caught a taxi."

"Don't be an idiot. I'm more than capable of giving you a lift home."

She smiled weakly. "I have cancer. I don't think you're allowed to call me an idiot."

"You really want me to start treating you like a patient?"

"No, you're right. I don't. Everyone else is treating me with kid gloves, I'd rather at least one person is normal."

He pulled over a spare chair so he could sit beside her. Everyone gave him a smile and nod of recognition, a strange kind of camaraderie that they were all in the same position, joined by the silent battle either they, or their loved ones, were going through.

"Have you heard from Dickhead?" he asked, referring to Donna's boyfriend, who had walked out on her after learning about her cancer.

"A couple of text messages, just asking how I am, but that's all."

"What do you think will happen when you're well again? Do you think he'll come crawling back?"

Donna let out a sigh. "Honestly, I don't have the emotional capacity to even think about that right now. I doubt he will, since I still won't be the person or future that he imagined, and it's not as though he's shown himself as a reliable, caring person, is it? Even if I was healthy, I'd know I wouldn't be able to rely on him sticking around if anything else happened."

He paused for a minute and then dared to ask, "Do you think that's what I did, after Hayley died, I mean. Did I do the same as Dickhead and ran the moment things got tough?"

"That was different, Ryan. For one, our marriage wasn't exactly filled with excitement and passion before we lost Hayley. But also, losing Hayley affected us both. We were both going through our own grief individually—we still are—and neither of us had the strength to prop the other one up."

He thought she was being too forgiving, but she was probably right. Hell, he still found getting through each day a struggle.

"I should have worked harder on our marriage before we lost Hayley. We didn't know how good we had it, did we? Really, we had the perfect lives, and we didn't appreciate it for a second. Instead, I was so overly focused on work, thinking that was the be all and end all, and that homelife was just an irritation that got in the way." She noticeably flinched. "Sorry, maybe I shouldn't have said that."

She shook her head. "No, I'm glad you did. We got into a rut, didn't we? Took each other, and having Hayley, for granted."

He forced a sad smile. "Guess it's true about not appreciating something until it's gone."

She reached out and squeezed his hand. "You make a better friend than you did a husband, Ryan."

"I have no idea if that's meant to be a compliment or not."

She gave a small laugh. "Let's not look into things that deeply."

Are you scared? he wanted to ask her but couldn't quite bring himself to form the words. If she admitted she was frightened, it would mean there was something to be frightened of—not only of dying, but also of there not being anything waiting for them afterwards. If there was nothing, then their daughter also went to nothing, and that didn't bear thinking about.

"How long's it got left?" he asked, nodding towards the bag of chemo that fed into the drip that went into the port. Donna had a port fitted into her chest which allowed the nurses to administer the chemo without having to find a vein each time. The unnatural shape of it beneath the thin layer of skin reminded him of something robotic.

"Not long. Should be done shortly. You can go and grab a coffee or something, if you want."

"Nah, I haven't got anywhere else to be."

"Rubbish," she scoffed. "I've never known you without at least five other things calling to you. How was work?"

"Crazy." He lowered his voice. "You seen the news lately?"

She shook her head. "No, I deliberately try to avoid it. My life's depressing enough."

"There were four murders in the early hours of Monday morning, all in one family."

Her eyes widened, and he knew she'd at least momentarily forgotten about her cancer.

"My God, that's terrible. Any idea who's responsible?"

"Can't say for the moment, but let's just say it wasn't a simple break-in. Things are more complicated than that."

They'd spent enough years married for her to understand what he was saying even when he wasn't saying it.

"How awful."

The machine she was attached to started beeping, and automatically they both glanced up towards the bag.

"Looks like I'm done," Donna said.

A smiling nurse came over. "All finished for today," she said. "Try to have something light to eat when you get home. Plenty of water and plenty of rest." She carefully took the tape of line going into Donna's chest. "Blow out for me."

Donna did as she'd been instructed, and the nurse removed the line. "You giving her a lift home?"

"I certainly am."

"Good." The nurse addressed Donna once more. "Take it easy for the next few days. Any worries, get in touch."

She gave a tired smile. "Thanks, I know the drill."

Ryan helped gather up Donna's belongings, and together they walked out to his car. She was slow and seemed to pick her footsteps carefully but refused to take his arm.

On the drive home, she sat in the passenger seat with her eyes closed and her head against the window. Ryan hated seeing her like this, but he knew she had it so much worse.

He parked in the driveway and carried her bag into the house. "I'll make you a cup of tea before I go."

She sank onto her sofa and fished the blanket off the back of it to wrap around her. Now she was having the chemo, she always seemed to be cold. "Don't worry, I've got Colette coming over after she's finished work. She's bringing me something to eat, too."

"Are you sure?"

"Yes, absolutely. I'm fine. You've already done enough."

He knew she was far from fine, and the next few days would be even harder on her already fragile body as the chemo did its job.

His phone rang. It was Mallory.

"I'm at the house with the SOCOs," she said, "going over everything with new eyes in light of what we learned from the post-mortems. Haven't found anything new yet. Just thought you'd want to know."

"Thanks. I'm with Donna at the moment."

"Oh, how's she doing?"

"So-so. She just finished chemo. I'm going to hang out here until her friend arrives to take over."

"Not a problem. I'll see you back at the office."

He ended the call.

"You don't have to stay with me," Donna protested. "I'm fine. Seriously, I'll probably just have a nap until Colette gets here and I have my phone, if there are any problems I can call."

He shook his head. "No, it's fine. I'll work later tonight to make up for it. It's not like I have anything I have to get home for." He turned for the kitchen. "I'll go and make that tea."

Chapter Eleven

"I think you're getting ahead of yourself, Helen."

Her husband stood with his hands folded across his chest as he took in the sight of the boxes stacked on the upstairs landing.

"Why?" she said. "It needs to be done."

"I know, but we haven't even sold yet."

Her husband's criticism of what she'd done rankled her. It wasn't as though he'd put in any hard work to get the house ready. He was always either at work or too tired, so it was all down to her. And yes, she knew he worked more hours than she did—especially now he had this new job—and he had the long commute to deal with as well, but things weren't exactly easy for her either right now. She would rather have his support than his criticism.

"And when we do sell," she said, "I want to be prepared. Do you have any idea how much crap we've managed to accumulate over the years, Andy? Seriously, this lot are filled just from the cupboards over the stairs."

He exhaled an irritated breath. "I'm just saying that it doesn't need to be done yet."

"Well, when will it be done, 'cause it's not as though you're here much at the moment to help out?"

"That's not my fault, Helen. It's the whole reason we're moving, remember? Why don't you get the kids to help out?"

She snorted—a sound that she realised was wholly unattractive. "I can barely get them to bring a cup down from their bedrooms. Do you really think they're going to start packing boxes? I just don't want to leave all of this to the last minute. Imagine if we sell to someone who needs to move quickly, and I haven't even made a start on packing and you're still away all the time? It'll be an absolute nightmare. I still have to work, on top of looking after the kids and packing up the house."

"So quit your job early. I know you want to. We'll manage."

"You know I can't. If we don't sell for six months, then we'll be stuffed financially."

"You mean you want to pack in case we sell early, but you also don't want to quit your job in case this takes months?" He let out a tired sigh and ran his hand through his hair. "I don't know what you want me to say or do, Helen. It's not like I can take time off from a job I've only just started."

She realised she'd got herself into a fluster and allowed herself to deflate. She'd been so stressed out lately—not that it was any surprise. "No, I know you're right. Just all this change has been a lot to take on."

"There have been a lot of changes for me, too."

Why did he always have to turn things into a competition? She wanted to say that his changes had been fun, challenging changes. He got to start a new job doing something he loved in street architecture and planning, and meet new people, and be wined and dined by his new employer. Yes, the commute was hard, but it couldn't be harder than being stuck in the house trying to deal with two mardy kids. But she managed to bite her tongue. It wasn't worth having an argument about, and life was stressful enough without them not talking.

"Actually," he said, "there is something I need to talk to you about."

Instantly, her stomach dropped. He hadn't told her what it was about yet, and she already knew she wasn't going to like it.

"My boss thinks I should stay down in Exeter a couple of nights during the week so I'm not having to do the drive every day. I got caught in traffic a couple of times last week and I ended up being late."

"What do you mean? In a hotel?"

"Don't worry, the company will cover the cost until we've moved."

"So, you're going to be away from home even more than normal?"

"You'll hardly notice. I mean, I'm barely home for a few hours in the evening anyway, and then we just go to bed and then I'm up at the crack of dawn to drive back down again."

She wanted to tell him that she wanted him to come home, but it would be childish of her. He was right—it was pointless him being back here for a few hours and leaving again. She liked having another adult in the house, though, and him coming home helped to break up her day. It was no fun sitting in the evening having a glass of wine in front of the television on her own, and Reese would rather be in her room chatting to her friends on FaceTime.

"And when is that going to start?" she asked.

"There's a meeting tomorrow night, so I'll stay over then, but I'll be back for the weekend."

"You're right, it's fine." She forced a smile. "It's only for a short time, anyway." *Hopefully.*

He pulled her in for a hug and kissed the top of her head. "I knew you'd understand."

Chapter Twelve

Amuffled cry from somewhere in the house had her awake in an instant. Mallory was out of bed before she'd even strung a thought together.

Ollie.

The shout came again, and she grabbed her dressing gown from a hook on the back of the door and threw it on. She caught a glimpse of her digital clock: 3:42. The tiredness hadn't hit her yet, she was surging on adrenaline, but she knew she'd feel it in a few hours when her alarm went off. She couldn't remember when she'd last managed to get a full night's sleep. A part of her wished she could sneak off to a hotel for just one night and leave her parents in charge, but she would worry that they wouldn't cope, and she'd probably end up getting even less sleep than normal. At least here, she was in her own bed.

She hurried across the landing and pushed open the door to her brother's room. He had a night light on in the corner, so it was easy to make out the shape of him sitting up in bed.

His eyes were open, staring at something she couldn't see. There was something eerie about it, as though another world existed that she wasn't privy to.

"It's okay, Ollie. It's just a bad dream. You're just having a bad dream."

Ollie didn't show any sign that he'd heard her. She approached the bed.

"No, I don' wanna—" He shoved an arm out as though he was batting someone away.

"Hey, it's all right, Ollie. I'm here."

She tried to remember the best thing to do when someone was sleepwalking. Not that he was properly sleepwalking—he hadn't even got out of bed—but he was clearly still trapped in his nightmare.

She sat on the edge of the bed and put out her hand to rub his back. "Ollie, you're just—"

He swung his right arm around, and a second later she was sprawled on her backside on his bedroom carpet. The shock was so great that at first she didn't even notice the throbbing of her eye and cheekbone, but as the heat bloomed, she realised what had happened.

Ollie had hit her.

He hadn't meant it—he hadn't even known she was there—but still the sense of hurt and betrayal swept through her. She gave up so much to care for him and now she was sitting on the floor in his bedroom in the middle of the night and she could feel her eye already starting to swell. Shit, how was she going to explain that away to her boss? She couldn't tell him, or anyone, the truth. They'd start saying that maybe she wasn't capable of taking care of Ollie and that perhaps she should look at him living somewhere else, but there was no way she was going to let that happen.

She choked back a sob and forced herself to clamber back to her feet. Yes, she was hurt, but Ollie was still trapped in his nightmare, and she was the only one who could help him. She approached him, but more warily this time. She'd never even thought about Ollie hurting her before—he was a gentle soul and he'd be so upset when he realised what had happened—but for now she had to be careful.

"Ollie," she raised her voice this time. "Ollie, it's time to wake up now."

He still seemed to be caught in his dream, thrashing his arms around. Did he think he was putting out the fire? A more horrible thought occurred to her. Or was he dreaming that *he* was the one on fire?

She wasn't going to leave him struggling. Her heart pounded, and she felt weak from pain and adrenaline, but she reacted without thinking. She was far more concerned about what Ollie was going through than herself. She knew this was going to take some thinking through, but now was not the time.

Sliding onto the bed behind him, she wrapped her arms around him and hugged him tight. "Hey, it's okay. You're okay. It was just a bad dream. You're safe now."

She had his arms pinned to his sides with hers, and he struggled against her for a moment. "I'm here, Ollie. Mallory is here."

His body suddenly went loose, and then he tensed again. "Mallory?"

He was awake.

"It's okay, I'm here," she continued to reassure him. "You were just having a nightmare."

"The fire." He let out a sob, and his body shook.

"I know, buddy. I know."

That bloody fire.

She'd been beating herself up about the fire ever since it had happened. If only she'd gone over what could be dangerous with him more often, or maybe told him not to use the toaster at all. If the fire hadn't happened, things would be easier for her, and Oliver would never have gone through the trauma of it.

She held him tight, letting the shudders work their way out of his muscles. Even as she sat there, she could feel her vision getting smaller as the skin surrounding her eye swelled, blocking it out. She needed to get some ice on it, but she wasn't going anywhere until Ollie had settled back down.

Ten minutes passed before he grew heavy in her arms and his breathing slowed and calmed. She edged out of the way, allowing him to lie back down while she perched on the edge. Ollie rolled onto his side, and she rubbed his back until she was sure he was asleep again.

She hoped he'd sleep through until morning now.

Cautiously, she got to her feet and slipped from the room. She was careful to avoid the mirror in the hallway, not wanting to catch sight of herself. It would be better after she applied some ice.

She went downstairs and walked into the kitchen. She found a clean tea towel and got some ice from the freezer and wrapped it up. Taking a seat at the kitchen table, she placed the ice to her eyes. Pain shot through her face, and she sucked air in over her teeth. She still didn't want to look at it, but she was going to have to before she went into work.

Mallory glanced at the kitchen clock. It was after four now. Was it even worth going back to bed? Would she sleep? She was worried she'd go to sleep and wake up and her face would be even worse.

She wasn't someone who wore a lot of foundation and concealer normally, but she was going to need it now.

Chapter Thirteen

The following morning, before heading back into the office, Ryan returned to the crime scene.

Because of the size of the property, severity of the crime, and number of victims, the crime scene hadn't yet been released, and SOCO—though in reduced numbers to what they had been initially—were still working on it.

Blue-and-white police tape was stretched across the front of the property, blocking access. He ducked under it and approached the front door where a bored-looking uniformed officer stood. The scene continued to be protected, both from reporters and sightseers and just kids who wanted to dare each other to enter the 'murder house'. The officer was young and probably the newest member on the force, hence getting landed with this job. At least it wasn't raining, but there was a chill in the air, and he had his hands stuffed into his armpits to try to keep them warm.

He took a more formal stance upon seeing Ryan.

Ryan held up his ID. "DI Chase. I need to take another look at the property."

"Of course." He stepped out of the way.

Ryan slipped on a pair of gloves and some protective footwear. He wasn't totally sure what he thought he was going to find this time around, only that he wanted to see the place with fresh eyes.

How could a building that seemed so normal from the outside have housed such horrors? Sometimes he did wonder about the number of places he drove or walked past on a daily basis that had hidden atrocities. He knew from experience that people did terrible things to each other all the time, and those were just the things they found out about. How many walls had seen things even he would find shocking?

He entered the hallway and paused for a moment, trying to see things through the killer's eyes. Would he or she have come in this way? They'd have been in full view of all the neighbours. No, more likely they came in through the back entrance and ran through to quickly disable the alarm. The rear door opened onto a small garden which had a gate at the far end that led onto a narrow alleyway. The search team had already worked that area, since it was clearly an escape route for the perpetrator, and had come up empty-handed. They'd checked the back alley for any CCTV, but unfortunately, there hadn't been any.

But Ryan wasn't there to find evidence right now, he was there to get into the head of the killer.

This house hadn't been chosen at random. Whoever the killer was had known the house, known the family. This had been carefully orchestrated.

He remembered how Liz Wyndham had reported that she'd thought someone had been watching the house, and that had been the reason they'd installed the home alarm. Maybe she'd been right.

Ryan inwardly chided himself. He should have got his hands on that report by now. He'd have to make sure it was first on his list when he got back into the office.

He stood in the back garden, taking everything in. How many people would have seen someone entering or leaving from this position? There was no additional lighting, so in the middle of the night it would have been dark. Even if someone had happened to look out of a window, it would have been unlikely the perp would have been spotted. The moon had been new, so there hadn't been any moonlight to help either. Had the killer timed it so that would be the case?

At the previous day's briefing, the findings of the post-mortem had been fed back to the team, including the SOCO coordinator, Ben Glazier. The findings about the family's final meal and them being drugged had put a new slant on what they'd been investigating.

There had been a slow cooker found in the kitchen, which could have been what the stew the family had eaten the night before had been cooked in. Unfortunately, it had also been washed up, but it had still been seized and was being tested for the drug diphenhydramine. The kitchen and outside bins had also been gone through for signs of food that might have been scraped off plates, but it appeared the family were all good eaters and there hadn't been any waste. Still, it made sense that the stew was the source of the drugs. If it had been slow cooked, it had been sitting on the side in the kitchen, most likely unattended, which would have given whoever drugged it ample opportunities.

His thoughts still went back to the possibility one of the victims had somehow been involved. It was the access to the house that kept throwing him. Who had access to the place on a regular basis? Did they have tradespeople coming in? A cleaner, perhaps?

Ryan switched positions, entering via the rear of the building. When he'd opened the back door, he would have set off the timer on the alarm, giving him thirty seconds to get to the front of the house and plug in the code to disable it. The problem was, there was only one time when the alarm had been disabled on the night of the murders, and that had been at 3.27 a.m., the time when the killer must have left, or else they'd have found him or her in the house with the victims, assuming the killer wasn't also one of the victims.

The killer was already in the house.

Ryan suddenly knew this was a certainty, as though someone had whispered the thought in his head.

They'd only disabled the alarm when they'd left, and then reset it again. There was no other time the alarm had been touched after that until the bodies had been found. Unless the killer had been someone in the house—such as Sheldon Wyndham—they must have left when the alarm had been reset in the early hours.

That was how they'd been able to move around the house and prepare it for the attack. They'd already been inside the property. They'd drugged the family via a family meal, knowing it would make them sleep deeply enough to allow them to do what was needed without being seen. Then they'd hidden somewhere in the house, waiting until the early hours, when they'd emerged, stolen and hidden the phones, trapped the kids in their rooms, and then went to murder Hugh Wyndham first.

Ryan ran his hand over his mouth, certain he was right.

But where would the assailant have secreted himself? This house wasn't huge, but it did have options. A large store cupboard was under the stairs. An airing cupboard housing a boiler on the first floor. Large built-in wardrobes. Maybe the killer had even been under a bed.

The idea sent icy fingers down Ryan's spine. He wasn't someone who spooked easily, but the thought of a killer hiding unnoticed in a house while the family went about their business, unaware of a stranger in their midst, was creepy as hell.

The windows in the house were all the same, and all of them were locked from the inside with a tiny silver key. There was no way the killer could have gained access to the house through a window, unless one had been left open, and he'd climbed through and then pulled it shut and locked it after him.

Ryan realised he was thinking of the killer as being male. That wasn't always the case, as he'd found out not so long ago with the Clara Reed case, and he needed to keep his mind open. He couldn't see a woman murdering a little girl, but it did happen.

He fished out his phone and called Mallory.

"I think the killer was already inside the house," he said before she could get a word in.

"What?"

"I think that's how they drugged them, how they knew where their phones were kept, and how they knew the alarm code. I think they were already in the house with the family, and they may even have been for some time."

"Do you mean without the family knowing about it?" she asked.

"Yes, I think so."

"Jesus Christ, that's terrifying. How were they not seen?"

"That part, I haven't figured out yet," he admitted. "There are plenty of hiding places. I'm going to get the Scenes of Crime officers to check obscure places like the inside of wardrobes and under beds for fingerprints and DNA."

"Would it have been someone the family knew, or a complete stranger?"

"Honestly, it could go either way at this point, but I feel like they must have known the house beforehand, otherwise how would they have known where to hide where they wouldn't be spotted? I also think they knew the family's routines."

"Didn't Liz Wyndham's friend say she'd been paranoid someone was watching the house and that's why she'd had the alarm installed?"

"That's right. I need to look at that report. But what if when she had the alarm installed, the intruder was already inside the house. Perhaps he or she even listened in on the instructions the alarm company gave them when they installed it?"

"You're giving me the chills."

"Yeah, I felt the same way."

Ryan glanced around. Was it even possible the perpetrator was still here? No, that was crazy thinking. The amount of police who'd swarmed over this place would have sent any killer running. Plus, the alarm had been disabled and reset at 3.27 a.m. That had been when the killer had left, via the back door, out into the garden and into the alleyway beyond.

Ryan remembered what Ben had said about finding traces of blood in the bathtub and bathroom. The killer had taken time to clean himself up, change his clothes or removed whatever he'd used to protect his own skin and clothing with. He had taken his time, but been thorough, and when he was satisfied with the clean-up, he'd casually disabled the alarm, reset it again, and left.

He'd treated this place like his own.

Ryan left the house via the back again. Would the killer have turned left or right from the back gate? Which way was less populated? Ryan tried both and discovered the road the lane came out on to the right had fewer houses—one of the buildings was a Chinese takeaway, the other a newsagent. If only one of them had had CCTV on the outside, not just inside. His officers had already questioned the shop owners, and no one had seen anything. Of course, they'd all have been shut at that time. Had the killer continued on foot, or was there a vehicle nearby that he'd used? Ryan wished there was a way of knowing for sure.

He needed to get his hands on that report.

Liz Wyndham had been paranoid about someone watching her. Could it have been the same person who'd somehow secreted themselves in the Wyndhams' house?

Chapter Fourteen

The office was its usual hustle and bustle. Ryan nodded morning greetings to those he made eye contact with and went to his desk. He sat and fired up his computer. He needed that report.

A few clicks on the mouse, and he was able to pull it up.

Liz Wyndham had kept a record of times and dates where she'd seen a white van across the street. She'd noted it down as being a Ford Transit, which she thought was fairly new, but she wasn't able to tell the year. Frustratingly, the report also said the number plate was always obscured in some way—whether it was with dirt or missing altogether. Considering she'd taken the time to report it to the police, the sightings hadn't been that often or for long. She'd recorded seeing the van twice the second week in July and again the first week of August and then twice again the week after. Each time, the van had driven slowly down the road, as though watching out for something, or else had been parked across the street, only to drive away once she'd noticed it. She hadn't given a description of who was driving, but thought it was a man on his own.

Ryan felt strangely disappointed. He'd been expecting for the sightings to have been more regular and numbered than that. If the van's plate hadn't been obscured, would Liz have even noticed the vehicle? Had the driver's attempt to make the van unrecordable ironically done the opposite? Could he even prove it had been the same vehicle?

There was something else. If whoever was driving the van had something to do with the Wyndham murders and used the same vehicle the night of their deaths, they were bound to have obscured the licence plate again. But if they were able to pinpoint a white van around that area on the night of the murders which had an obscured licence plate, Ryan thought he would be able to say with reasonable confidence that it was both the same van that Liz had reported and so would most likely belong to the killer. Having the number plate would go a long way to finding the driver, but it wasn't the only thing that could be used to recognise it.

They couldn't have done that all the time, though, without eventually getting pulled over and questioned by the police. Considering what they'd been planning, Ryan imagined that was the last thing they'd have wanted. But they might well have scoped out the area with the plate visible on other occasions.

He spotted Mallory sitting at her desk, her black hair over one side of her face. He wanted to bounce his thoughts on that morning's discoveries off her, so he slipped out of his chair and approached her desk. It occurred to him that she hadn't said hi to him when he'd come in either.

"Morning," he said, eyeing her curiously.

"Morning," she replied, still not looking up. Instead, she put her elbow on the table, her fingers pressed to her temples, so her palm shielded her face.

It was clear something was wrong.

"Everything okay?" he asked.

"Of course, why wouldn't it be?"

"You're hiding your face."

"Yes, I am," she admitted. "I had a bit of an accident during the night."

He folded his arms. "Show me."

She lowered her hand and lifted her chin, and he did his best not to suck in a breath of shock. She'd clearly tried to cover up the bruising with some makeup, but it hadn't helped, and makeup couldn't hide the swelling or the way she could barely see out of one eye.

"Jesus, Mallory. How did that happen?"

She rubbed the side of her nose. "I got up in the night to get a drink from the kitchen and turned and smacked my face against the cupboard door in the dark. It was a stupid thing to do. I put some ice on it. I'm sure it'll be better by the end of the day."

He highly doubted that. He also doubted her story. Hit it on a cupboard door? How many times had he heard that before? He recognised a punch when he saw one.

But who would have hit her? She hadn't mentioned a boyfriend being in her life—not that it was any business of his who she dated. He'd make it his business if she had hooked up with someone who treated her like that, though.

He lowered his voice. "Mallory, unless someone held the back of your head and slammed your face into a cupboard door, I highly doubt that was how your injury happened."

She didn't meet his eye. "Well, it did."

"You should get it checked out by a doctor. You might have a fractured cheekbone or eye socket or something."

"I know my own body," she said. "I think I'd know if something was broken. It looks worse than it is. And anyway, we have a big case to work on. It's not like I can take time off."

"Yes, you can, if it's something serious."

"I promise, it's not."

"If you're working, Mallory, I want your head in the job. I don't want you distracted or worrying about whatever is going on with you."

"Nothing's going on with me. I'm fine."

She was stubborn as hell, and he knew he wasn't going to change her mind. "Okay, but any headache or dizziness and you get straight to the hospital. Got it?"

She nodded. "Got it."

He was already running late for that morning's briefing, so he called everyone together in the briefing room.

"First thing's first," he started, "I believe whoever killed the Wyndhams may have been driving a white Ford Transit. Liz Wyndham reported one with a concealed number plate across from the house a couple of months before the killings. Craig, you're still working the CCTV from the area?"

DC Penn nodded, his shoulders sagging. "Yeah. There's a lot of it."

"Any white vans caught your eye?"

Craig arched an eyebrow. "This is Bristol. Every other vehicle is a white van, especially with everyone online shopping these days."

"I need you to check all the traffic cameras around the area between three and six a.m. on the Monday morning and make note of them all. I want every vehicle registration checked, and if you find one that doesn't have a licence plate or has an obscured plate, we're going to need as many close-up images of it as possible."

"You think our killer might be driving it?"

"I'd say it's unlikely to be a coincidence."

Craig frowned. "That report was from months ago. You think whoever did this had been planning it for that long?"

Ryan was annoyed at himself for not investigating it sooner. "I do. Maybe they hadn't been planning to murder the family for that length of time, but they knew about them and were already watching them."

"Do you think it's someone who was already in their lives or someone random?"

"At this point, I'm not sure how they came into their lives or what their involvement was, but I think they knew the house."

Knew it well enough that they were able to move around it freely and without the family being aware.

"I'll get onto it right away," Craig said.

Ryan addressed the rest of the room again. "I also believe the killer may have been in the house before the family went to bed that night, which is why the alarm history is only showing as being disabled and armed once during the night, which is when the killer must have left. If they were concealed in the house, they must have known the layout of the building to know where to hide, so I think the perp was known to the family or at least to the house. They also had time to drug the family's food that evening, which means they had the opportunity. Did the Wyndhams have someone over for dinner the evening before they died?" He looked to Linda Quinn who had been interviewing the neighbours. "Have any of the neighbours reported seeing someone else going into the house?"

Linda shook her head. "Frustratingly, no one saw anything. However, one of the neighbours did say she heard Liz and Hugh arguing a few months ago. Their house is the one that backs onto them, just across the access alley that runs behind the property." Linda checked her notes. "She described the argument as being 'intense'."

Ryan pursed his lips. "But no one else has mentioned the couple having any marital issues?"

"No, they haven't, but you know what people say about things that happen behind closed doors."

Ryan rubbed his thumb against the corner of his mouth and then instantly thought about what kind of germs he might have put there. "Might just be a one-off. All couples fight from time to time." He and Donna used to have horrendous fights before they eventually just gave up and fell into avoiding each other instead.

"Yes, but not all couples end up murdered in their beds."

Ryan considered it for a moment. "Unless the neighbour can give us some idea about what the fight was about, it's not much good to us. Let's focus on finding out who had regular access to the house."

"Yes, boss."

"What about the family's final movements on the Sunday? Where are we with that?"

One of the detectives they'd pulled in from another division replied, "It was just a normal Sunday, as far as we can tell, though without any of the actual family to interview, it's hard to know for sure. Liz Wyndham used her debit card in the local Sainsburys for what appears to be the usual weekly shop at eleven twenty-six on Sunday morning. Hugh Wyndham went to the local newsagents and picked up a paper shortly after nine a.m., according to the shop owner. We can't find any reports that either Dulcie or Sheldon went anywhere that day, so they may have spent their final day in their rooms, which probably isn't unusual for teens and pre-teens these days."

"Anything on any calendars, either online or paper in the house, that mentions someone going for dinner that night?" Was that even something people wrote down these days?

"Not that we've found."

He focused on his DS and tried not to be distracted by her injury. "Mallory, what about the phone records from Conrad Smales? Do we know if his story about turning his phone off matches his normal pattern yet?"

"It's not something he does regularly," she said, "but yes, he has been known to turn it off for periods of time, and according to the tracing on it, the phone was at his home address during the times he says."

"He works for a transit company, though. Can you check and see if they use Ford Transit vehicles?"

"From what I've seen during my visit there, it's all huge lorries rather than vans, but I'll double-check."

"Right now, Conrad is the only one with a motive who knew the family well enough to have access to the house to drug them, but him working during that day makes things complicated."

Ryan dismissed the briefing, and everyone dispersed back to their desks or left the office to follow up on their action.

DCI Hirst hadn't been in the briefing, as she'd been caught up in another case, so he went to her office and knocked on the door. She called for him to come in, and he pushed the door open and stepped inside.

Mandy Hirst gestured for him to take a seat opposite her desk. "Any solid leads yet?"

"I wish I had more to tell you, but we're still working on it. I believe the perpetrator is someone who had access to the house, however, and they may have been driving a white Ford Transit. We don't have any solid witnesses, which is frustrating, and we're still working on the CCTV footage from the area. I don't believe any of the victims had anything to do with the murders."

"Any thoughts on motive?"

He shook his head. "Other than a very tenuous one to do with the ex-husband, I'm afraid not. Why someone would want to murder an entire family is still a mystery, though I think it was someone they knew, someone who even had access to the house."

"Surely that must narrow it down?"

"We're still looking at Sheldon Wyndham's biological father, Conrad Smales, but he was working during the hours leading up to the killings. As far as we're aware, the family were all going about their normal business on the Sunday, we haven't discovered anything unusual in their pattern, which meant they hadn't even left the house by the time Smales was already on the road."

"So, he wouldn't have had time to drug the evening meal," she said.

"That's right. He potentially had time to leave the depot and kill the family, but it would be cutting it fine." Ryan paused and said, "There's one other thing, too. I believe whoever killed them was already in the house when they went to bed that night, which means there's no way it could have been Smales."

DCI Hirst blinked. "Already in the house?"

"Yes, ma'am, like hidden away somewhere."

"Any idea where?"

"Not yet. I've got SOCO still working on the house, checking secluded places like the inside of wardrobes and under beds for fingerprints. We might get lucky and come up with prints that don't belong to any of the family members. If we can match the owner of the fingerprints to a white van owner somewhere in the area, then we might be onto something, but there's a lot of 'ifs' in that statement."

It had been more than forty-eight hours since the murders, and Ryan was fully aware that the longer it took them to catch the killer, the greater the chance would be that they'd never find the person responsible.

Chapter Fifteen

As Ryan left his boss's office, a desk sergeant approached him.

"DI Chase, there's a girl in reception asking for you."

Ryan frowned. He hadn't been expecting anyone. "For me? By name?"

"Well, no, she's asking for whoever is in charge of the Wyndham murders. She says she has information."

"Did you catch her name?"

"Elouise Lewis."

It didn't ring any bells either.

"Okay, thank you. I'll be right down."

Ryan finished up what he was doing and then went down to reception. His gaze flicked over the people sitting waiting but didn't recognise any of them. He glanced over at the reception desk sergeant, who nodded to the corner where a tall girl with mousy brown hair sat with her legs crossed, her head bent over her phone.

"Elouise Lewis?" Ryan said.

The girl lifted her head, an awkward smile flashing across her face before it transformed back into a worried frown. She got to her feet, shoving her phone into her pocket and slinging her bag over one shoulder. She gripped the strap with the opposite hand, creating an unconscious line of defence between them. Ryan guessed she was somewhere between the ages of sixteen and seventeen, but it was hard to tell these days. All girls seemed to look older than they actually were.

"I'm DI Chase," Ryan continued. "Can I help?"

She glanced around. "Is there somewhere private we can talk?"

"Of course. I will need to bring an appropriate adult in to sit with us though. Since you haven't come with your parents, I assume they don't know you're here."

"No, they don't. Please don't tell them."

One of the police constables was passing through the reception area and Ryan flagged him down. "You okay to sit in on an interview with me," he asked. "Shouldn't take too long."

The PC nodded. "No problem."

"Great. Come through." Ryan addressed Elouise. "I'll find us an empty interview room."

He led them both through the doors and down the corridor, wondering what this was all about. He'd dealt with enough time-wasters in his career, and he hoped this wasn't going to be another one. Interview room three was empty, so he punched in a code and let them both in.

He gestured for her to sit while the constable stood by the door. "What can I do for you, Miss Lewis? It is Miss Lewis, isn't it? Elouise Lewis?"

She nodded. "Yes, that's right."

He jotted it down. "Can I take your current address and date of birth as well."

She told him and he noted the street was the same as the Wyndhams'.

She peered around nervously. "I wanted to talk to someone about what happened to the Wyndhams."

"Did you know them?"

She nodded. "I'm their neighbour—I *was* their neighbour."

"Okay, and you think you might know something about what happened to them?"

She focused on her hands twisted together on the table. "I-I'm not sure. It probably has nothing to do with what happened and it's all just so awful—" She broke down, and Ryan waited patiently for her to gather herself again.

"If I tell you something," she asked, "will it become public knowledge?"

Ryan's gut instinct told him that this girl had something she was ashamed of. She was closest in age to Sheldon. Could there have been a secret relationship between the two of them?

"I mean, that completely depends on what you tell me. I'm not a solicitor or a doctor. We don't take a Hippocratic oath or anything. If you tell me something that's of use to the case, then I'll have to inform my colleagues, and if it becomes vital to a conviction, you may have to testify in court. But there are things we can do to protect your identity, especially as you're under eighteen."

She nodded. "That's what I hoped you'd say." She swallowed hard. "I don't even know if it's going to make any difference, but I couldn't keep it a secret. It's been eating me alive, thinking maybe someone found out and this was their punishment, though why they'd hurt the others, I don't know. And I'm scared, too, 'cause what if it is because of that, and whoever killed them is planning on coming after me next?"

"You're going to have to explain what you mean, Elouise. Find out what?"

She seemed to gulp air. "I was having an affair."

"An affair? With Sheldon Wyndham?" It seemed like an old-fashioned way of phrasing it.

But she almost whispered, "No, with his dad."

"With Hugh Wyndham?"

"Yes." She covered her face with her hands. "Oh my God, I'm such a cliché. I babysat for Dulcie a couple of times when Sheldon wouldn't do it 'cause he was busy, and so Mrs Wyndham—Liz—asked me if I'd like to watch her for some extra money. Hugh saw me home a couple of times, and my parents weren't in. I'm sure I don't have to explain the rest to you."

So, the perfect life of the Wyndhams hadn't been so perfect after all. He wondered if the affair had been the reason one of the other neighbours had heard Liz and Hugh arguing. Was Hugh a serial adulterer, or had this just been a one-off? Either way, the age difference was enough to make the whole thing feel unsanitary.

"Did he force himself on you at all?" Ryan asked.

"No, he wouldn't do that. I know it probably doesn't sound like it, but he was a nice bloke. He was only ever kind to me, even after I told him we couldn't carry on doing what we were doing."

The girl was seventeen. Although morally wrong, she was old enough to consent under UK law, and Hugh wasn't in a position of power, such as being her teacher. It wasn't as though they could prosecute him now, even if he had been.

"When did your relationship with Hugh start?"

"About six months ago. It wasn't a relationship. I mean, I know I called it an affair, but it was just a couple of times of stupid fumbling. I knew he was way too old for me, but he said all the right things, about how he thought I was pretty, and I was so much more mature than other girls my age. I stopped it, but the damage was done by then. I guess that's why they decided to move."

He frowned. "They were going to move?"

"They were going to start afresh somewhere new. I don't know if Liz found out about us, or if Hugh was worried that she would, so he convinced her it was a good idea. I just know within a week of me telling him we couldn't do this anymore, there was a for sale sign in the garden."

Ryan lifted a finger. "Hang on a minute. They went as far as putting the house on the market?"

"They'd been planning to go to Australia."

There hadn't been any for sale signs in the garden that Ryan had noticed, and no record that the house had been sold recently. The friend of the family hadn't even mentioned it, and neither had any of the neighbours. He could only imagine it had been a flash in the pan, and no one had thought it would be relevant.

"So why didn't they go?"

"Sheldon, I believe. He refused in the end. Said they'd have to kidnap him in order to get him on the plane. I think he even asked his dad if he could go and live with him, but his dad didn't want him there, which probably broke the poor kid's heart. So, in the end, they just thought they could wait a few more years until Sheldon was old enough to look after himself. Of course, then Dulcie would have been in her teenage years, and they probably would have hit upon the same problem with her."

Fucking hell, why had no one mentioned this before?

"Did his wife find out about the affair?"

"I think she might have, or at least been suspicious."

The interviews they'd done with Liz Wyndham's friends hadn't mentioned there being any issues within the marriage. Had Liz kept it a secret, even from her friends? Or had she suspected but never had proof? Did everyone just think Liz was being paranoid again?

"Did Liz confront you at all?" he asked.

"No, but they stopped asking me to babysit, which I thought was telling enough, and then there was the for sale sign, though it wasn't up for long."

There was the chance none of this had anything to do with the murders, but it did create a motive. Had someone wanted Hugh dead because he'd seduced the babysitter? But then why had they killed the whole family? Had things gone wrong, and they'd had to kill the rest of the family to cover up what they'd done?

Or did none of this have anything to do with what had happened?

Either way, he had no choice but to consider Elouise Lewis as a suspect. She had motive, and even if she hadn't committed the murders directly, she might have had an accomplice.

"You know that you're entitled to have a solicitor present while you're talking to me, Elouise. We can provide one for you."

She frowned and shook her head. "I don't need a solicitor. I haven't done anything wrong."

"I'm not saying you have, you just need to know your rights." It was time he read them to her. "You do not have to say anything, but it may harm your defence if you do not mention when questioned something which you later rely on in court. Anything you do say may be given in evidence."

She nodded and looked down at her hands. "I understand, but honestly, I'm here to help. I haven't done anything wrong." Her cheeks coloured. "I mean, apart from getting involved with Hugh."

"Does anyone else know about what happened between you and Hugh?"

"No, I didn't tell anyone. I was embarrassed, to be honest. I know I shouldn't have done it."

"What about your parents? Did they have any idea?"

"God, no. Just the thought would be mortifying. My dad would have killed him." She must have realised what she'd said as she clapped her hand over her mouth. "I didn't mean that. It's just an expression. My dad wouldn't hurt anyone, and he definitely wouldn't have murdered the whole family like that." Her eyes welled with unshed tears. "Poor people."

Even though she'd said her father didn't know about what had been going on, Ryan still jotted down 'Mr and Mrs Lewis' in his notepad. It wasn't going to be an easy conversation to have, but he didn't have any choice. He imagined if his daughter had lived and got to the age of seventeen, and he found out the forty-something-year-old neighbour had seduced her, it would have been enough of a reason for him to want to go and beat the son of a bitch senseless. Just the thought made anger rise inside him, and Hayley had been dead for years. But that was where the violence would have stopped. He never would have taken a father away from his children, and he certainly wouldn't have killed an entire family for the father's mistakes.

Elouise's eyes widened. "You're not going to have to tell him, are you? Please don't. I never would have come here if I'd thought you'd tell my parents."

Ryan let out a sigh and thought for a moment. "How about if I just go and talk to them? Find out where they were the night of the murders, ask your parents' thoughts on Hugh, test the waters? That kind of thing."

Her voice was small. "Okay."

Linda would have already spoken to the family, but now they had this new information, it would be done with a new slant. Even if Elouise's father did have an alibi, it wouldn't make him completely innocent. Maybe he'd paid someone else to kill Hugh Wyndham but then Liz woke up and the person ended up taking out the whole family to cover his tracks.

But no, that didn't fit in with the preparation that was done beforehand—the removal of the mobile phones and jamming the chairs under the bedroom doors to prevent the children from getting out. Whoever killed the family had planned to do so from the start.

"Where were you the night of the murders?" he asked her.

"At the cinema with friends until about eleven thirty, then I came home and went to bed. My parents can vouch for me."

"How well do your parents know the Wyndhams?"

She shrugged. "Just like most neighbours, I guess. They say hi, and take in each other's post, that kind of thing."

"Would you have said they were friends?"

Her face crumpled. "I didn't come in here to point the finger at my parents. They're innocent. I just wanted to help you find whoever did this to that poor family."

"And I appreciate that you did. You've given us a fresh insight into Hugh Wyndham. Maybe there were others—who knows—but at least now we know to look. And I realise this is difficult, but please understand that we need to rule out any possibilities and that's all we're going to be doing—ruling your parents out. Like you said, they're innocent, so there's nothing to worry about."

Elouise sniffed and wiped at her eyes. "Can I go now?"

"Of course."

He'd never forced her to be there—she'd been there purely of her own free will—and yet she'd felt the need to ask. Some people just had a natural inbuilt respect for authority, and he wondered if that was what made her so susceptible to Hugh Wyndham's advances. He'd been older and, since she'd been babysitting for him, he was also in a way, her boss.

"Oh," he stopped her, "one more thing before you go. Did Hugh ever contact you by phone?"

"Yes, but it's just a cheap pay as you go. My parents wouldn't let me have a contract after I ran up a huge bill one time. He phoned me and messaged me all the time while...it was going on."

"Can I take your phone number? I need to cross it off a list."

He handed her his notepad and pen, and she jotted it down. He was fairly sure that when he cross-checked it with the mystery number Hugh had been calling a few months ago, it would be the same one.

Ryan saw Elouise out of the building and then got on the phone.

"Mallory, where are you?"

"I've just been to Conrad's place of work to ask about those Transit vans."

"Any luck?"

"No. Like I thought, they're all big lorries here. Smallest one has twelve wheels."

At some point, he was going to have to cross Conrad off the list of possible suspects. He knew he was holding back because once he did that, he was left with no one.

"Okay, thanks for checking. I need you to go around to the Wyndhams' street and speak to one of the neighbours, Mr and Mrs Lewis at number forty-eight, and reinterview them both."

"What's going on?" A combination of interest and concern was evident in her tone.

He lowered his voice slightly. "Their daughter, Elouise, has come in saying she had an affair with Hugh Wyndham, six months ago."

"Shit. So, they weren't the perfect family then. You think this might be a revenge killing?"

"Honestly, I'm not sure. But can you play things carefully? Get an idea about what they thought of Hugh and put some feelers out about the relationship, without actually coming out and saying it. The daughter really doesn't want them to know about it, and I've told her we'll do our best to be subtle unless we really have no choice."

"Of course. I can be subtle."

Ryan paced up and down the corridor. "Find out how much they knew about the house. There's a chance they would have known the alarm code." He was about to end the call and then remembered something else Elouise had mentioned.

"Oh, one other thing. Did you know that the house was on the market a few months ago?"

Mallory's voice came down the line. "No, that didn't come up anywhere."

"Yeah, it was only for a short time. Sheldon kicked off about it, and they changed their minds. They'd been hoping to emigrate to Australia. Ask them about it. I don't know if it was because of the affair, but the house went on the market not long after it had ended. Maybe the Lewises weren't happy when the Wyndhams changed their mind about moving, and they decided to take a different route to getting new neighbours."

"Like murdering the whole family?" she suggested.

"That's what we need to find out."

Ryan ended the call and thought about the Wyndham family. They'd been dreaming of another life down under—sunshine, white sandy beaches, and barbeques—but something had changed that. He considered it wistfully.

They should have gone.

Chapter Sixteen

Mallory left the lorry depot and drove to the Wyndhams' street. She'd been happy to get away from the haulage company. Peter Phipps hadn't exactly been pleased to see her again.

Was Ryan right about his idea that someone was already in the house when the family had set the alarm for that night? It did make sense, but the thought of someone hiding in the house while the family went about their business was unnerving. That it ended in their brutal murder was even more chilling.

The news of the affair changed things. If Elouise's parents found out about the affair, would it have been enough of a motive for them to want Hugh dead? She couldn't imagine having a seventeen-year-old daughter, but if Elouise's father had seen Hugh as an equal and then discovered he'd taken advantage of his teenage daughter, she could see how that might make someone murderous. But even if they planned to murder Hugh, why had they killed the rest of the family? The wife and children were innocent. The only thing she could think of was that they were trying to cover their tracks, but it must take a cold-hearted son of a bitch to commit a crime like that.

She pulled into the road and found a parking spot not far from the house. The Lewis house was a couple of doors down from the Wyndhams', so they hadn't been adjoining neighbours. They'd obviously known each other well enough, though.

The police presence remained strong on the street, with the Wyndham house still being a crime scene. A handful of reporters hung around as well, hoping to pick up on a part of the story the other papers might have missed. They all turned to her as she climbed out of her car, but she slammed the door shut, and hit the button to lock the vehicle, and then briskly walked away from the Wyndham house and towards their neighbours'. The reporters must have been from out of town as they clearly didn't recognise her and perhaps thought she was just someone who lived locally. She ignored their calls of 'excuse me'.

She walked up to the Lewis's front door and rang the bell.

A couple in their late forties to early fifties answered the door. They both seemed tight-lipped and anxious, as though they were expecting bad news. She guessed having an entire family murdered right next door was enough to leave anyone paranoid.

"Mr and Mrs Lewis?" Mallory asked, holding up her ID. "I'm DS Lawson. I wondered if I could have a word?"

The couple exchanged a glance with each other.

"Oh," Mrs Lewis started, "we've already talked to one of your lot. A DC Quinn."

Mallory smiled, conscious of her swollen eye. Was it really noticeable? Would it make the couple less likely to trust her if they saw she was injured? Would *they* start asking *her* questions? She hated to think someone might think she was a battered woman.

"Yes, that's right," she said. "We have some follow-up questions. I'm sorry to take up more of your time, but as I'm sure you're aware, this is a big case, and sometimes things need to be gone back over."

Mrs Lewis took a step back. "Well, I suppose that's okay. You'd better come in then."

Mallory entered the house. "Thank you."

They showed her into the living room, and everyone sat down.

Mrs Lewis folded her hands in her lap. "It's terrible what's happened. I can hardly believe it. I keep playing over the thought that we were all sleeping in our beds peacefully, completely unaware of what was happening just a few doors away. They must have been so frightened." She paused and bit her lower lip. "I'm not sure what more I can tell you that I didn't tell the other detective, though."

"I'll probably have you repeating yourselves," Mallory said, "but it really is all part of the process, so please just be patient with me." She turned her head to address Mr Lewis. "How well did you know the Wyndhams?"

"Fairly well, as far as neighbours go. We've been living on the same road for what"—he glanced to his wife for her backup—"six years now?"

Mrs Lewis nodded. "Yes, about that. We had kids that were around the same age, so it was only natural for us to get friendly."

Mallory checked her notes. "Elouise, is that right?"

"Yes, it is."

"How well did she and Sheldon know each other?"

Mrs Lewis pulled a face. "Well, Elouise was in the year above Sheldon, and when you're a teenager, that year counts, if you know what I mean. Plus, Sheldon wasn't exactly the sort of person that Elouise hangs around with."

"So they weren't friends?"

"No, they weren't. She got on with Darcie better. She used to babysit for Darcie occasionally."

"Did she?" Mallory said, as though this was news to her. "How often did she babysit?"

"Not very often." Mrs Lewis shrugged. "A couple of times a month, at the most."

Mallory wrote that down. "When was the last time she babysat?"

"Oh, gosh, I can't remember." Mrs Lewis turned to her husband. "Can you, sweetheart?"

Mr Lewis ran his hand over his mouth. "It was a while ago. At least six months, I think."

Mallory studied him for any change in body language, any hint that he might be hiding something, but he remained relaxed.

"Was that normal," she asked, "for her not to have babysat for so long?"

He frowned. "Now you mention it, it had been some time, but I assumed that was because Dulcie was getting older. She just started secondary school, so she probably thought she didn't need babysitting anymore."

"That's understandable." She focused on Mr Lewis. "How well did you get on with Hugh Wyndham in particular?"

Was there any reaction? A flicker of guilt or anger? But no, it was more confusion flooding his expression than anything else.

"Fine, but it's not as though we were friends."

She kept pressing. "Did you have any reason to go over to the Wyndhams when Elouise was babysitting?"

He frowned. "No, not that I can think of."

"But you have been in their house before?"

One side of his mouth turned down. "I mean, maybe briefly. It's not like we spent time in each other's houses or anything."

Mallory frowned and pretended to check her notes again. "What about when they went on holiday. Did they ever ask you to keep an eye on the place? Water the plants, that kind of thing?"

Mrs Lewis spoke up. "Oh, that was me more than my husband. You know how these things are. Always left to the women."

Mallory smiled. "Of course. Did they give you a key when you needed to water the plants?"

"Yes, but I gave it back again as soon as they returned from holiday."

"They didn't want you to hang onto one for them? Sometimes neighbours hold onto each other's keys in case they get locked out."

"No, they obviously didn't feel the need to do that."

Mallory nodded. "And how did Elouise get on with them? Did she ever mention any arguments happening between the Hugh and Liz?"

The couple exchanged another look.

"No, I don't think so," Mrs Lewis said.

"What about between Elouise and Hugh or Liz?"

Mr Lewis's eyes narrowed. "No, why would they have argued?"

"Just asking a question," she said brightly. "Trying to ascertain the relationship between you all."

Mrs Lewis put her hand on her husband's knee as though silently telling him to be calm. "She got on with him fine, as far as I'm aware. Like I said, we all did."

Did Mr Lewis have a temper? Was his wife aware of it, and the hand on the knee was her way of telling him not to let it show in front of a detective?

"Good, that's good." Mallory folded her hands in her lap. "Now, let's get back to the night of the murders. You were home?"

Mrs Lewis nodded. "Yes, it was just a normal Sunday night. We had a roast dinner, which I always like to do on a Sunday, watched a bit of television, and went to bed."

"Together?" Mallory checked.

They exchanged another confused glance. "Yes, of course together," Mr Lewis said.

"What about Elouise? What did she do that evening?"

Mrs Lewis frowned thoughtfully. "Oh, she was out at the cinema until about eleven thirty. She caught the bus home and went to bed as soon as she got in."

"And what happened in the morning?"

Mr Lewis continued. "We got up, I went to work, as did my wife, and Elouise went into college."

"You didn't have any idea something terrible had happened across the street?"

"God, no," Mrs Lewis said. "It wasn't until Elouise got back from college and saw all the police, and then she phoned us both at work, that we had any idea they were all dead." She pressed her knuckles to her mouth. "It's so awful, us all going about our normal days while their bodies just lay there."

"But you didn't see or hear anything unusual?"

Mr Lewis was getting irritated. "We keep saying that we didn't."

Mallory switched angles. "What about a white van on the street? A white Ford Transit in particular. Has there been one that might have caught your eye? Think back, even over the past six months or more."

Mrs Lewis shrugged. "There are always white vans around, especially now everyone gets everything delivered. I don't think a day goes by when there isn't one at some time during the day."

"Did Liz Wyndham ever mention thinking that a person driving one was watching her and the house?"

"No, never."

Mallory remembered the question Ryan had wanted her to ask. "Did the Wyndham's ever talk about wanting to move to Australia? I believe their house was on the market not so long ago."

"We saw the for sale sign go up, but then it was practically down again the next day," said Mrs Lewis. "They never mentioned anything about wanting to move abroad to me, so I guess it was one of those impulsive things that they changed their minds on again pretty quickly."

"Was there anything else?" Mr Lewis interrupted. "We really do have to get on."

Mallory had asked everything she'd planned to. She rose and brushed down the front of her suit trousers.

"Of course, I'll leave you in peace." She plucked a card from her pocket and handed it to Mr Lewis. "If you think of anything you haven't mentioned here today, please, pick up the phone."

He nodded and gestured towards the door. Mallory obliged, heading out, but paused before she reached the front door.

"Oh, one last thing," she said, turning back to them. "Did the Wyndhams ever give you the code to the alarm system when you were watering the plants?"

She shook her head. "They didn't have an alarm system installed then. That's a more recent thing."

"Right. Thanks again for your time."

Mallory left the house and kept her head down, not wanting to make eye contact with the lurking reporters. She trotted to her car, fished her keys from her jacket pocket, and hit the button to unlock the doors. She slid behind the wheel and took out her phone and called Ryan.

"How did it go?" he asked when he answered. "What are your thoughts on the Lewis family?"

"We can't rule them out completely since their only alibis for the night of the murder are each other, but I didn't get any hint that they were hiding anything. They said they hadn't needed to look after the house since Liz put the alarm in, so they had no idea what the code was."

"But then they would say that if they'd used it to murder the family."

"True. I just didn't feel they were trying to hide anything—at least nothing that extreme. Mr Lewis got a bit terse when I was asking about the relationship between them all, but I'm not sure if perhaps he suspected there might have been something more between Hugh Wyndham and Elouise, or he just didn't like the implication that he might have known more about the murders than he was letting on."

Ryan didn't respond for a moment, and then his sigh came down the line. "Okay, can you check with the other neighbours, find out if there were ever any rumours going around about a rift between the two families? Also see if there's anyone else who saw the Lewises around the Wyndham house before the murders."

"Will do, boss."

Mallory's stomach told her it was lunchtime. She could spare twenty minutes to get a bite to eat. The neighbours would have to wait.

Chapter Seventeen

Ryan grabbed an hour at lunch to take Donna some soup and see how she was doing. As expected, she was feeling rough. He found her curled up on the sofa, a blanket around her shoulders, and a woolly hat pulled down over her naked head. It was always hardest for her in the days that followed the chemo; the nausea and pins and needles in her hands and feet were all-encompassing.

"I hate that you're living on your own," he told her after he'd decanted the soup into a bowl and placed it on the coffee table in front of her. "What if something happened and you weren't able to call an ambulance?"

"I'm fine, Ryan. I'm having chemo. I've not suddenly reverted back to toddlerhood."

"I can move back in for a while," he offered. "I could take care of you."

She gave him a derisive look. "Seriously, do you think you living here would be any good for either of us? There was a reason you moved out."

Deep down, he was relieved. As much as he had no emotional connection with his crappy flat, it was his own space that he could do whatever he wanted in. The last thing Donna needed was him wandering around all night, checking and rechecking doors and windows, and keeping her awake. She'd notice and ask questions of him that he didn't want to answer.

It would only worry her, when she already had enough to worry about. Plus, he had no idea how he'd react to being back in the house again and if it would flare up his OCD. He'd had it under reasonable control recently, and he did everything he could to manage it. He was already feeling the pressure of this case, the frustration of not getting anywhere, and knowing the killer was still out there. Everyone expected him to catch the bastard.

"Okay, you're probably right," he admitted, "but you know the offer stands if you change your mind."

"I won't change my mind."

What if the chemo doesn't work? What if you keep getting sicker? Who's going to take care of you then?

He didn't voice his concerns. She wanted—and needed—to stay positive about this journey and the last thing she needed was him writing her off already.

"At least Hayley never had to see me like this," Donna said.

That took him aback. "Don't say that."

"Well, it's true, isn't it?" She gestured at her head. "I probably would have terrified her."

"Donna, you wouldn't have terrified her. She loved you, and would have continued to love you, maybe even more because she would see how incredibly strong and brave her mother is."

Donna blinked back tears, and Ryan's chest tightened. Donna wasn't a crier, or someone who wallowed in self-pity, so she must be feeling really low to be thinking like this. He also wasn't great with anyone when they were upset, especially about something as serious as this.

"Can I call one of your friends? Get them to come and sit with you?"

She sniffed and wiped at her eyes. "No, I'm fine, honestly. Sorry, I don't know what came over me."

"You're allowed to cry, Donna. You're allowed to feel angry and sad, and scared, and everything else you're feeling. Your daughter died, you got cancer, and your dickhead of a boyfriend left you." He didn't add, 'and your marriage broke down'. "Anyone dealing with just one of those things would have the right to cry, never mind all three."

"It's been a long time since Hayley—"

"That doesn't make it any easier. Missing her will always be a part of you." He risked a smile. "I'm not sure about crying over Dickhead, though."

The small joke paid off, and she smiled back. "I wasn't crying over him."

Maybe she was telling the truth right now, but he was sure she'd shed some tears, no matter what Ryan thought of her ex.

"I have to get back to the office. Are you sure you're going to be okay?"

"Yes, go. I know you have a big case. I have my phone to get in touch if I need anything. And thank you for the soup. Hopefully, I'll be able to taste it."

The chemo had done strange things to her tastebuds as well. Sometimes, it seemed to Ryan, that the cure was as bad as the cancer.

He leaned down and kissed her forehead, and then let himself out of the house. It felt strange being back. Even though it wasn't his home any longer, and hadn't been for some time, it was hard not to feel as though he still belonged there.

As he approached his car, his phone rang.

"DI Chase," he answered.

"Ryan, hi, it's Townsend."

It was the detective who'd been in charge of his daughter's case after the accident. His stomach dropped, a rush of cold flooding through his veins. Just hearing the other man's voice felt like he'd fallen back into that time when both he and Donna were fresh in the moment of trying to figure out how they were supposed to exist in a world without their daughter.

"How are you?" Ryan asked. "Is everything all right?"

"I felt I should keep you informed about something."

"What's that?"

"Cole Fielding woke up yesterday. I thought you should know."

His knees went, and he found himself grappling for the roof of his car to keep himself upright. "He woke up? I thought that wasn't going to happen."

"It was always a possibility. An unlikely one, but a possibility nevertheless."

A vision of himself standing on a bridge flashed through Ryan's mind. It was night, and the roar of a river rushed beneath him. He squeezed his eyes shut. No, that wasn't right. It wasn't a memory. It was another intrusive thought. He hadn't had anything to do with what had happened to Cole. Had he?

If it was me, Cole will be able to say exactly what happened now.

Being unconscious, Cole had never been able to give a statement of his own. The police just had to put together the pieces—the note he'd left, a guilty conscience, the rope tied to the bridge. But if he was awake, he could tell the police about the events that landed him in hospital.

It should be a relief. If Cole was able to confirm the police's suspicions, then Ryan's fear he had been responsible would be dissipated. He'd know for sure that he hadn't done something to the young man, however much he might have thought and fantasised about it.

Ryan opened his car door and climbed behind the wheel, before slamming the door shut behind him again. He didn't think there was much chance of Donna overhearing the conversation, especially since she was pretty much tied to the couch, and if she saw him talking on the phone, she'd just assume it was a work call, but he wasn't going to risk it.

"Is...is he talking?" Ryan dared to ask.

"He's simply conscious at this point. I'm not sure he's going to be capable of talking, after everything he's been through."

"What *he's* been through?" The turn of phrase made Ryan incredulous, and a familiar surge of anger rose inside him.

"Sorry," Townsend said. "You know what I mean."

Did Ryan feel relieved at that news, or not? If there was a possibility that he didn't do what he feared, wasn't it better to know for sure? But what if he was responsible for what had happened?

No, you were home that night, he told himself. The neighbour confirmed it. When he'd gone and asked about a car being scrapped, the owner of the garage had shaken his head and said, nope, no car had been brought to the garage to be scrapped. But was that just because Ryan had told him the whole thing was never to be spoken of again, and being a police officer, the garage owner had thought it had been some kind of test Ryan had been putting him through.

Besides, while he had wanted to know, he also hadn't wanted to say or do anything that would incriminate himself.

Ryan reminded himself that he was the good guy. He hadn't been the one to run over a little girl and then flee the scene of the crime and hide out until his blood alcohol levels had dropped enough to prevent him getting a death by dangerous driving charge.

Ryan tried again. "He hasn't been able to say what happened to him then?"

"No, not yet."

"Is it possible he'll be able to at some point then?"

"Honestly, Ryan, I don't know. I'm not a doctor. They said it would be unlikely he'd ever wake up, but the family wanted to hold on, not wanting to give up on him. God knows why, we could do with one less murderous piece of shit in this country, if you ask me."

Ryan agreed with Townsend.

"All I ever wanted was for him to spend the correct amount of time in prison for killing Hayley. We all knew he'd been drinking that day and then he got behind the wheel of that car. The judge got it wrong that time. He should never have been out from behind bars for that...incident...to ever have happened."

"I can't say how much I agree with you, Ryan. This must be so hard for you, and for Donna, too, knowing he's on the road to recovery after what he took from you."

Ryan's stomach dropped for a second time. Shit, Donna. What was he going to do about Donna? He needed to think about that. She had so much on her plate right now, getting news like this could really set her back.

Ryan cleared his throat. "Listen, Townsend, is there any way we can stop this news from reaching Donna? She's having chemo right now and the last thing she needs is to have to worry about that arsehole on top of everything else."

"Oh shit. Yeah, of course. I mean, I can't stop her hearing it from outside sources, but I promise it won't come from me."

"Thanks, I appreciate that."

Ryan ended the call, threw his phone to one side, and sat with his head in his hands. His thoughts were a whirling dervish of worries and fears, his heart knocking against his rib cage. He found himself counting his fingers, placing his thumb to each one in turn, starting at his index finger, moving to his middle and on to the next.

One, two, three, four... One, two, three, four.

Over and over, he counted, until his heart finally slowed, and his thoughts calmed.

What was it that had upset him so much? Was it the news that Cole Fielding was on the road to recovery, or was it his fear of the truth finally coming out?

Chapter Eighteen

It took Ryan longer than he would have liked to admit to pull himself together enough to go back into work. This wasn't what he needed while he was in charge of such a high-profile case. He needed to focus on work, but his brain was pinging with anxiety. He wanted to find out just how awake Cole Fielding was, but other than going to visit the other man in hospital, he couldn't see how that was possible. He toyed with the idea of going in and using his status as a police detective to get past the gatekeepers of the nurses and doctors, but that wouldn't exactly be ethical.

Right now, he was needed at work. He spent the afternoon following up on where each of his team were with their actions. The phone number flagged on Hugh Wyndham's phone was traced to Elouise Lewis, supporting her story. Ryan still hadn't written off the Lewises as potential suspects, but he also couldn't allow himself to be fixated on them when he had no proof to back up his suspicions.

Mallory had spent several hours interviewing neighbours again, but this time with the slant of there being issues between the Wyndhams and the Lewises, but had come up empty-handed.

He was trying not to worry about Mallory, on top of everything else. Had she met a bloke who wasn't treating her right? She hadn't mentioned going on any dates—but then was that something she'd talk to him about? She'd never been much of a dater, as far as he was aware, mainly because she didn't have time. She always had her hands full with either work or taking care of her brother. But he'd been around the block long enough to recognise an injury when it had been caused by a fist instead of a cupboard door, as she'd claimed. He made a mental note to keep an extra eye on her.

Towards the end of the day, a phone call came in from Ben Glazier, the SOCO coordinator.

"Tell me you've got some news," Ryan said wearily.

"I've got some news."

Ryan straightened in his seat. "Tell me."

"We've matched the hemp and wool fibres found at the crime scene. They're from blanket insulation."

"Insulation? Like the kind found in the walls of houses."

"Or found in lofts," Ben said.

"Lofts? Shit." His theory the perp had been hiding somewhere in the house while the family went to bed hadn't been far from his mind. "That's where the killer was hiding. They must have brought some of the insulation fibres down on them when they attacked the family."

"That's what I'm thinking as well. I've got officers searching the space again now. We checked it initially for anyone hiding there and nothing appeared out of the ordinary, but now we'll look at it with fresh eyes."

"Are you at the property?" Ryan asked.

"Yes, I am."

"I'll be there in thirty."

TRUE TO HIS WORD, HALF an hour later, Ryan was pulling on protective outerwear and climbing a ladder into the loft space of the Wyndhams' house. Being over six feet, he had to duck and half crawl to avoid hitting his head on the wooden struts that held up the roof, but then he was able to straighten into the highest point where there was enough head height. Floodlights had been brought in to illuminate the otherwise dark space, and he spotted fluffy yellow insulation material poking through the roof structure. Brushing against it would easily transfer fibres onto skin or clothes.

Two other people shared the loft space with him. One was Ben Glazier, and the other was a female Scenes of Crime officer.

"Found anything?" Ryan asked Ben.

"Nothing obvious, but we're dusting for prints. Watch where you're stepping. It would be easy enough to go through the ceiling if your foot slips."

To move around the loft, he had to step from rafter to rafter, careful where he put his size ten feet.

From between the rafters, a flash of silver caught his eye. He stopped and with a gloved hand, bent to pick up the item. It was wedged beneath the wood, squashed against the insulation, so had been easy to miss—he would have missed it if he hadn't been watching where he was stepping. He pulled the item back up and placed it into an evidence bag.

"What do you make of this?" He held the bag up.

Ben frowned. "A fork? What would a fork be doing in the loft?"

"Someone must have brought it up here. Maybe they dropped it and didn't realise. What reason would someone have for bringing a fork up here other than using it to eat with, and if someone has been eating up here, I'd say they were here for more than just a few hours."

"You think someone has been living in the loft?"

Ryan expelled a breath. "I think it's a possibility. We might get lucky and be able to get a DNA sample or prints from the fork."

Ben took the bag from him. "I'll get it submitted as evidence ASAP. Let's keep our fingers crossed."

"I'll keep everything crossed," Ryan said. "We could use a breakthrough on this case."

Chapter Nineteen

That night, Ryan checked his front door was locked—as was his usual ritual—and went to the bathroom. He brushed his teeth, stripped down to his underwear, and got into bed. He lay there, staring at the ceiling, his thoughts tumultuous. He should be focusing on the case right now, turning over every possibility about who had murdered the Wyndham family, but instead his thoughts were with Cole Fielding. He wished he never had to think about that son of a bitch ever again, and instead his head was full of him.

He squeezed his eyes shut and counted backwards from one hundred, trying to stop his racing mind.

If Cole woke and thought that Ryan had something to do with what had happened to him, would he come after him? Would he think Ryan had taken out his revenge and put him in a coma? Would he be wrong?

A second thought crept in. *Did I lock the front door?*

Yes, he had. He remembered doing it.

Do I remember locking it, or is that a memory from last night?

It was just an OCD thought, and he knew from his research into his condition that he should just acknowledge it for what it was and move on. But the trouble with the intrusive thoughts were that once they'd entered his head, they wouldn't go away again until he'd given in to them. It was like waking during the night and needing to use the bathroom—the feeling wouldn't go away until he gave in and went.

With a huff of exasperation, he threw back the bedcovers and crossed through the flat. He reached the front door and yanked up the door handle. It was locked.

"For fuck's sake," he muttered.

Then the window locks started beckoning him. Had he locked those, too? When was the last time he'd checked them? The flat was on the ground floor, so anyone who wanted to slide open a window and climb in could, if it wasn't locked.

Now the thought had come to mind, he had to go around to each window and jiggle the handle to ensure they were all locked. Satisfied they were, he took himself back to bed. It was half past midnight now, and he needed to sleep. He shut his eyes but couldn't seem to get them to stay shut. They pinged open, and he found himself staring at the ceiling and watching the moving shadows cast from the lighting outside.

Did I lock the door properly?

Ryan groaned and jammed the balls of his hands into his eye sockets.

No, no, no.

He needed to ignore the thoughts. It was the only way to deal with this. He couldn't keep giving in every time. It was like having restless legs, a constant twitching and niggling that refused to go away.

If the door's open, someone could just walk right in. Cole Fielding could start talking and send people in here to take revenge on you.

He wasn't afraid of Cole Fielding. It was the opposite way round—Cole Fielding should be the one frightened of him coming to finish off the job.

I didn't do anything. It was an intrusive thought.

The moment he'd heard that Cole Fielding had tried to hang himself off a bridge, but that it had failed, and he fallen into the river below and almost drowned, resulting in his being in a coma, the thought that he was the one responsible had entered Ryan's head and had refused to leave. He'd experienced intrusive thoughts before, but none had been so real. He felt like he had actual memories of what happened, but then at the same time, they also felt distant and blurry around the edges, like he was remembering a dream.

I need to get up and check the door.

Furious with himself, he got up and repeated the process, checking the lock an exact number of times. Four. His safe number.

With everything done, he took himself back to bed. He glanced at the clock again. It was after one now. The hours were ticking by. He had to get some sleep.

He took himself through all the mindfulness exercises he'd self-taught to try to deal with his issues, breathing exercises, meditation, picturing himself at the top of a tall staircase with a beautiful garden below, and slowly counting the stairs as he walked down them. But the moment he started counting, he kept needing to do it in blocks of four, and then the counting to four made him think of the front door again.

He needed to go to sleep, but the voice in his head wouldn't rest.

You didn't lock it, you didn't.

I did. I checked it already.

No, you flicked it the wrong way. You opened it instead of locking it.

He grabbed a pillow and jammed it down over his face, roaring his frustration into the cotton and feathers.

He had to check.

With gritty eyes, he looked at the clock. Almost two a.m. Dammit. He had to be up in four hours to get into work. This was never going to end. He'd be going back and forth until his alarm went off.

He threw back the bedcovers and stormed through the flat. He wrenched on the door handle, and it came as no surprise to him that it was locked.

"Fuck!" He slammed both fists against the wall. "Fuck, fuck!" He punctuated each curse with another drum on the wall.

He was forty-six years old, and he wanted to sob like a baby.

A tentative knock came at the door, and he sniffed and straightened, pulled out of his cycle and self-pity.

A small voice came through the wood. "Ryan? Is everything okay in there?"

Shit, it was his eighty-year-old neighbour, Mrs Furst. He must have woken her with all his noise.

"I'm fine, Mrs Furst. Really."

"I don't believe you, Ryan. Open the door."

He didn't have much choice. "Umm, hang on a sec."

He grabbed a t-shirt that had been left on the back of his sofa and tugged it on. He knew he must look a state, his dark hair sticking up all over the place, his blue eyes bloodshot and puffy.

He opened the door to his neighbour standing in their shared entrance hall.

"Is everything okay?" she asked. "I heard shouting."

"Sorry, I had some bad news today."

"What kind of bad news?"

Where should he start? That someone had murdered four people and it was his job to find out who and he didn't have the foggiest? Or that his ex-wife had cancer? Or that the bastard who'd killed his daughter was finally waking up?

He went with the latter.

She listened to him and then patted his hand. "Wait here."

He didn't know where she thought he was going to go, considering this was his flat, but he watched her bustle back out the door. She returned a moment later with a bottle of expensive whiskey in one hand and two glasses in the other.

"Seems to me like you could do with one of these."

He normally tried to control his drinking the same way he tried to control everything else, but she was probably right, and at this point, what harm would it do.

"Why not?" He gestured to the coffee table, and she placed down the booze and the glasses and took a seat on the single armchair.

"You can be mother." She nodded to the whiskey.

He took that as she expected him to pour, so he uncapped the bottle and poured them a good finger each. "Sorry, I don't have any ice or anything."

She scoffed at him. "What? To water down a good whiskey with? Sacrilege." She picked up her glass and tilted it to him. "Cheers."

He clinked his glass to hers. "Cheers."

He wasn't sure he had much to be drinking to, but the alcohol felt good as it burned down his throat and the heat punched him in the diaphragm.

"So," Mrs Furst said, settling back in her seat, "are you going to tell me a bit more about what's been going on with you? I hear you at night, pacing back and forth."

"I'm sorry." He frowned. "Am I keeping you up?"

"I'm not much of a sleeper either, to be honest. Haven't been for a long time. A few hours at night, and an hour or so nap in the day seems to be enough for me."

"I see."

"What is it that bothers you so much about this man waking up? Had you hoped he wouldn't?"

"Perhaps. It doesn't feel right for him to go on having a life when he stole Hayley's away from her before she ever got the chance to live it."

"That's understandable. He stole a lot from you as well. The opportunity of watching your daughter grow up, maybe even to have grandchildren one day. It's normal to be angry."

Ryan rubbed his hand over his mouth. "I'm a police officer. I'm supposed to trust in the system, to believe that a person will serve the correct amount of time for the crime they've committed. But he didn't. He might as well have walked for the small amount of time he spent behind bars. That's what makes me so angry, and what makes me think I might have been—" He cut himself off, realising what he'd been about to say—*I might have been capable of trying to kill him.*

"Capable of taking things into your own hands," she finished for him.

He glanced up at her and nodded.

"You don't seem like the type of man who is capable of hurting another person," she said.

Ryan chewed on his lower lip. "I thought the same, but now I'm not so sure. After my daughter died, it did something to me. The rage I felt was like nothing I'd ever experienced, and I started to question what kind of person I was."

She took a sip of her whiskey. "The kind who'd lost his only daughter. Something like that is bound to change a person. I'd have been surprised if it hadn't."

The urge to confess everything built up inside him. It would feel good to purge himself to another person, to empty his head and heart of all the thoughts and feelings that had mounted up over the years and months since his life had fallen apart. He'd considered talking to Donna about it, but before now, she'd been with another man and he hadn't felt it was his place, and now she had cancer to worry about without him piling on all his problems as well. Besides, he wouldn't put either of them in such a difficult position. If Cole Fielding did start talking one day and pointed the finger at Ryan, his own colleagues would be around asking questions, and he didn't want either his ex-wife or neighbour to feel they had to lie to protect him.

He lifted his glass to his lips and downed the rest of his whiskey. "I should really try to get some sleep now. I've got to get up for work in the morning."

"Yes, of course. I won't keep you any longer. Hope you manage to get some sleep." She got to her feet and picked up the bottle of whiskey. "I'd tell you to keep this, but I'm not that generous."

Ryan chuckled and saw her out, bidding her goodnight.

He shut the door behind her and sighed as he turned the key to lock it once more, knowing he'd have to repeat the action another three times before he could go back to bed.

Chapter Twenty

Fifteen-year-old Reese Bolton jerked awake, her heart racing. She half-sat, and her gaze flicked to her phone. She reached out a shaking hand to swipe the screen to display the time. It was just gone two-thirty. What had woken her? Had it been a nightmare?

Her heart was still racing, but she couldn't pin down the reason. The room was in darkness—the only light coming from a gap beneath the door. The landing light was left on, something her parents had always done when they'd been little, so they'd be able to get to the toilet and back again without being scared and feeling the need to wake their parents. Of course, they'd been old enough to find their own way to the toilet at night for many years now and were no longer scared of the dark, but the habit of leaving on a night light had stayed.

A shadow passed under her door.

She stiffened. It must be one of her parents or her brother. But she could hear her dad snoring in the other room, and she hadn't heard the click of one of their bedroom doors opening either.

Had she imagined it? A leftover from her dream or nightmare, or whatever had woken her?

What if whoever is out there is what woke me?

She closed her fingers around the smooth glass and metal of her phone for reassurance. All it would take was a swipe of the screen and she could call nine-nine-nine. Hell, she could open her mouth and scream, and her parents and her brother would come quickly enough.

Her imagination was running away with her. All she'd seen was a brief shadow. It could have been anything.

The self-reassurance helped to calm her, and she took a couple of breaths. Now she was awake, her bladder was making itself known to her. She shouldn't have drunk that extra glass of water before going to bed. Could she ignore it? She knew it was going to be harder to fall asleep when she was thinking about needing to go to the toilet. At least if she went, she could put her mind to rest about there not being anyone else in the house.

That didn't help at all.

There's no one out there. You're acting like a kid.

She slid her legs out from beneath the covers and planted them on the floor, her toes curling into the soft carpet. The thought of there being someone—or something—beneath her bed flashed through her imagination. Jesus, what the hell was wrong with her tonight? She was completely spooked and for no good reason. No one was out there. She'd heard her dad lock up the house before he'd come up to bed, just the same as he did every night.

She'd worn her knickers and an oversized t-shirt to bed, so at least she didn't need to worry about encountering a burglar when she was naked. She shook her head at herself. If she actually encountered some stranger, would she really give a shit about what she was wearing?

Her hand trembled slightly as she reached for the door handle. She was being ridiculous, but she'd spooked herself now and couldn't seem to shake it.

Just get to the bathroom, pee, and then get back to bed.

Sucking in a breath, she edged open the door and peered out.

Aside from her mother's stacked pile of packing boxes, the landing was empty.

She strained her ears, trying to pinpoint any sound that didn't belong. Every house had its own noises, even when its inhabitants were sleeping. A click of pipes. The whistle of a draughty window. The creak of a floorboard shifting.

The rhythmical snoring from her parents' bedroom continued. Reese was glad her dad was still home. Tomorrow night, he'd be staying down in Exeter, and it would just be her, her brother, and her mum here.

It was only a short walk to the bathroom—just a matter of a few steps—but she would have to cross the top of the stairs. What if someone was there, hidden just out of sight?

She was tempted to turn around and climb back into bed again and try to ignore her bladder, but then she gave herself a shake. She was being an idiot. She stepped up to the top of the stairs, and, with her heart in her throat, peered down into the stairwell.

She exhaled a breath. It was empty. She'd just been letting her imagination get away with her. Reese crossed the rest of the landing, navigating the boxes, and entered the bathroom. She reached out to pull on the cord light and tried to block out any mental images of someone grabbing at her hand. She still hadn't quite shaken the feeling of there being someone after her, and she was thankful they had a clear glass shower screen rather than an old-fashioned shower curtain that might have harboured someone lurking behind it.

Once she'd relieved herself, she finished up, quickly washed her hands, and stepped out again, clicking off the light. The paranoia she'd been experiencing had subsided somewhere mid-flow, and she crossed the top of the stairs on the way back to her bedroom.

A flash of movement darted to her left, a dark shape blocking the light at the bottom of the stairs.

Reese let out a shriek, and she lurched forward, falling over her own feet.

Her father's snores stopped abruptly, and a second later her mother appeared in the doorway.

"Reese? What's going on? What's happened?"

Was that the click of the back door shutting that she heard, or something else?

"I-I think someone was in the house?"

Her mother's eyes widened. "What?"

"I heard something. It woke me up, and I thought I saw movement under my door. When I came out to check, I decided to use the toilet, and then on the way back I was sure I saw someone run past the bottom of the stairs."

Her dad had appeared behind her mother now, his eyes red from sleep, his face puffy.

"Can you go and check downstairs, Andy," her mother said, her face creased with concern. "Reese thinks she might have seen someone."

He raised his eyebrows. "Seriously? The house is all locked up."

Her mother placed a hand on his arm. "Please, just check. It'll at least put our minds at rest."

"Are you sure you haven't just been watching inappropriate things online," he chided Reese. "You spooked yourself out watching some horror film on Netflix?"

"No, Dad, I haven't, I swear it!"

He huffed out a breath of irritation, clearly unhappy at having his sleep disturbed for what he took to be something she'd imagined. But she hadn't imagined it, had she?

He still didn't budge. "Do you know what time it is? I have to get up early in the morning."

She cringed. "Yes, Dad. It's not my fault."

"Can you just go and check, Andy," her mother said, starting to get impatient.

"Fine."

In just his boxer shorts, he stomped down the stairs, clearly not expecting to find anyone at all. Reese didn't think any intruder would be overly worried at coming across her dad in his underwear with his slight potbelly straining over the top of the waistband. Even so, she did feel better knowing he was going to check.

"Be careful," she called after him.

He moved around downstairs, turning on each light, opening and shutting doors. When he'd finished going through the house, he walked back up the stairs towards them.

"Did you check the back door was locked?" Reese asked.

"Yes, of course. It was locked, just as I'd left it."

"What about the front one?"

"That, too. Everything is normal, Reese. You need to go back to bed now. Hopefully, we can all get a few more hours' sleep. It's a good thing you didn't wake your brother up as well."

"Sorry, Dad."

He didn't say anything else but took himself back into the bedroom.

Her mother was a little more sympathetic. "You think you'll be able to sleep?"

"Yeah, I guess so."

"Good. I'll see you in the morning."

She vanished back into her bedroom, and Reese slunk into her own room and shut the door firmly behind her. She got into bed and pulled the covers up but didn't switch off the light. She doubted she'd be able to go back to sleep tonight, and if she did, she definitely didn't want to wake up in the dark, imagining someone standing over her.

Chapter Twenty-One

Helen hadn't appreciated the alarm going off that morning. More than anything, she'd wanted to turn it off and roll back over and forget she'd ever heard it, but, as usual, she had things she needed to do.

She wasn't the only one who was up early. Andy needed to leave before seven in order to be in the Exeter office by eight-thirty, and she realised his side of the bed was already empty. For a moment, she thought he'd left even earlier than normal, eager to get away from their household, but then she heard the distant thunder of the shower running. She hoped he'd been able to sleep after Reese had woken them up for her wild goose chase.

She let out a sigh and threw back the covers. Her dressing gown hung on the back of her bedroom door, so she grabbed it and wrapped herself within its soft folds, and then stuffed her feet into her slippers. She needed to wake the kids for school. Reese was going to be even harder than normal to wake this morning after their nocturnal shenanigans, and, with her being a teenager, she was a nightmare at the best of times. At least Tyler hadn't been disturbed, so hopefully she'd only have one grumpy child to deal with.

She walked out onto the landing and drew up short. Something was off. She was sure the stack of boxes that contained the packing she'd done so far had moved about a foot to the left. Had they been like that when Reese had woken them during the night? She couldn't remember. She'd been more focused on her daughter than worried about the boxes.

Her husband exited the bathroom in a billow of steam, a small towel wrapped around his waist. She tried not to wince. It really was far too early in the morning to see quite so much of his growingly rounded body.

"Andy, did you move those boxes?" she asked.

"No, why would I want to move your boxes?"

Helen wanted to protest that they weren't exactly *her* boxes, since they contained stuff that belonged to all of them, but she didn't.

"I'm sure they've moved. Not far, but just a bit to the side."

"Are you sure you're not just imagining things. Maybe you moved them and forgot. I mean, it's not like they've been moved far. Perhaps one of us just bumped up against them and they slid across the carpet."

Maybe she had been imagining things. Or she'd moved them herself, though she couldn't think why she'd have done that. "No, they're too heavy to have moved by someone bumping them."

It was such a little thing, it seemed stupid to get hung up on the position of a few boxes, yet it had left her uneasy.

"Maybe one of the kids dropped something behind them," he suggested, "and had to move them to get it."

"Do you really think they would have done that without complaining about it to us first? And like I said, they're heavy. I'm not sure they could have done it on their own."

"There's only one way to find out for sure. Let's ask them."

"They're both still asleep. They're not going to give us a straight answer."

"Well, maybe you need to wake them up then. Shouldn't they be getting ready for school by now? Which reminds me, I need to get into work, or I'm going to be late." He took a couple of steps and paused again. "And don't forget that I'm staying in Exeter tonight. I've got that big meeting."

"Right. I remember."

He brushed past her, leaving her to deal with the kids, and she tried not to focus on the spike of resentment that went through her. Andy would be dressed and out of the house within fifteen minutes, while she'd be left battling with Reese and Tyler, all while trying to get herself ready and to work on time as well. At least there weren't any viewings arranged for today. If she had to worry about how tidy the house was before they all left on top of everything else, she thought she'd lose her mind. Of course, that there weren't any viewings didn't speak well for their chances of selling.

Helen decided to tackle her son first and went into his room. She opened the curtains—not fully, but enough to let in some light. "Come on, kiddo. Time to wake up. You've got school to go to."

Tyler groaned and pulled the covers over his head to block out the light.

Helen tugged them back down again. "Come on. Up you get."

"Five more minutes."

She hardened her tone. "No, now."

Helen left her son's room and went to her daughter's, bracing herself. Reese had a sharp tongue that she used to lash out without thinking about who she hurt or the consequences. Sometimes Helen felt as though she was in a constant battle with her daughter, and it was exhausting.

But when she opened Reese's door, she was surprised to discover her daughter already sitting on the edge of the bed, fully dressed, applying mascara to eyelashes that didn't really need it.

"Oh, you're up already."

"Yeah, I couldn't sleep, so I figured I might as well do something useful." She plugged the wand of the mascara back into the tube. "What were you and Dad talking about with the boxes?"

Beneath the makeup, dark shadows under Reese's eyes told of her sleepless night.

"I'm sure it's nothing," Helen said, not wanting to worry Reese further.

"I heard you ask him if he'd moved them."

"If you heard me, why ask what you already know?" Helen said, exasperated.

"Do you think the man I saw last night might have done it?"

Helen blinked in surprise. "What? No, of course not. There was no man. Your dad checked, remember?"

Reese bit her lower lip. "Yeah, I remember."

Helen lowered herself on the edge of the bed next to her daughter. Where Reese was normally all brittle barbs, there was something more vulnerable about her today. The whole incident must have really shaken her up.

"Honey, this house is safe. It's all locked up at night. No one was in here."

"So you keep saying."

Helen didn't know how to convince her daughter that everything was fine, but she really didn't have time to sit around debating it. She didn't even think Tyler had got out of bed yet.

From downstairs, Andy called up. "I'm off now. See you tomorrow."

"Bye," she shouted back, but her soul felt heavier. She was on her own now until at least Friday night. It wasn't even seven a.m., and she was already exhausted.

Chapter Twenty-Two

"You look shattered," Mallory said, sliding a large coffee from one of the local cafés onto Ryan's desk.

"Thanks, I am." The knot that had appeared in his stomach ever since getting the news about Cole Fielding still hadn't abated. "Didn't get much sleep last night."

"How come?"

He didn't want to admit the truth. "Neighbours kept me up." It was kind of what had happened, after all.

She raised an eyebrow. "Isn't your neighbour eighty?"

"She knows how to party."

Mallory laughed. "Good for her."

Ryan couldn't bring himself to tell her about Cole Fielding. Besides, without her knowing the real reason behind his fear about Cole waking up, she wouldn't understand his reaction anyway. He was sure she'd be sympathetic—after all, the man had killed Ryan's daughter—but taking her sympathy would have felt like a lie. Like it was something he didn't deserve.

His thoughts had been with Cole Fielding far more than they should have been. He hadn't heard anything more from the detective who had worked the case, and he hadn't wanted to get in touch for fear of appearing guilty. He told himself that if Cole was talking and he was guilty of anything, he would have heard about it by now. So, did that mean Cole wasn't talking? Or did it mean Ryan was innocent?

The two possibilities battled in his mind, forcing out other thoughts. His OCD was raging, too, and he had to keep his hands in fists at his sides to prevent himself straightening up Mallory's desk, which looked as though a teenager had been working at it. How she could focus under such conditions was beyond his comprehension, but some people thrived in chaos, and he'd worked with her long enough to know if he asked for something, she'd be able to put her hand on it in an instant.

He felt as though if he knew if Cole Fielding was talking then it would put his mind at rest. He could either prepare himself for the truth coming out, one way or another, or he could stop worrying about it.

Cole Fielding had been in the Bristol Royal Infirmary since his 'accident'. It angered Ryan that the NHS was having to fund the bill for that son of a bitch's care, but then the public would also have been funding his prison stay if Cole had got the length of prison sentence he should have had. The other option would have been for Cole to have gone on to live a normal life, and just the thought filled Ryan with fury. That man had taken Hayley's life and hadn't even seemed sorry about what he'd done and the lives he'd destroyed. Ryan was sure Cole would never have been someone who would turn his life around. He'd have probably hurt someone else and ended up back behind bars.

"HAVE WE GOT ANYTHING else from the loft yet?" she asked.

"The fork is still being processed. SOCO found fingerprints, too, but whether they belong to the killer, or just to the family or even builders, we're yet to find out."

"It could be a big breakthrough if we can get a match. Your instincts on someone already being in the house were right."

He nodded slowly. "Looks that way. What concerns me is where is the killer now? I still feel as though he—or she—was someone who already knew the house and the family's routines well, which most likely means it's someone known to them. I just wish I could pin down who."

DC Craig Penn approached his desk, and Ryan was glad to have the distraction.

"Boss, I've been working on this practically all night, and I've tracked down several white Ford Transits that were caught on camera in the area after the time the house alarm was reset."

Ryan sat up straight. He hoped this was going to give them a real lead.

"Good work. Have you narrowed any of them down?"

"Not yet, I'm still working on it. Three of them are registered to businesses, so I'm going to need to find out exactly who was driving them at that time. If they can prove they were in a different area or have an alibi during the time of the murders, so before three thirty a.m., then we can strike them off the list."

"Excellent."

"One of the vans is registered to an individual," Craig continued, "so I'm trying to track him down. No luck yet."

"Keep me updated, and pull in another detective to help, if you need it."

He hoped this was going to lead to something. A part of him was still kicking himself that he hadn't taken Liz Wyndham's earlier police report more seriously, while the other part niggled that he could be wrong, and Liz Wyndham had just been paranoid. The white van might have had nothing to do with the killer. Even so, this was a lead he'd be an idiot not to follow. It wasn't as though they were drowning in them.

He called that morning's briefing to fill everyone in on the developments from the previous day, and made sure Craig had additional help finding the drivers of the Transit vans. He put Mallory on to chasing up forensics about the DNA or prints that might have been found on the fork, and then slipped out of the office.

Chapter Twenty-Three

Ryan stood in the entrance of the hospital. People walked past him in both directions, some carrying flowers and balloons, others with their heads down or side by side with their arms around each other's shoulders. A couple of people sat in wheelchairs, and hospital porters wheeled patients past on gurneys.

Maybe he shouldn't do this. He could turn around right now and walk out, but his feet felt glued to the floor.

Was Cole likely to have anyone with him? Any family who cared? There hadn't been anyone with him in the courtroom—or at least no one who'd owned up to being related to the man who'd killed an innocent little girl and then called the family of that same girl wankers for fighting to make sure he paid for what he did. Maybe he had someone out there who still loved him, but Ryan saw things in more black and white than that. Someone who'd do such a thing wasn't deserving of love.

Ryan considered lying about who he was to gain access. He could say he was Cole's uncle who happened to be in the city and wanted to drop in on his sick nephew. Maybe it would backfire on him if the nurse told someone he'd been in to visit Cole. Would the nurses even recognise his name as being the father of the girl Cole had killed? Did they know what Cole had done? Did it matter to them, or did they treat him just like any other patient?

First, he had to get to the ward Cole was on, and then he'd take things from there.

With his heart thumping, and dizzy with adrenaline, he made his way through the hospital. He paused outside the double doors for the correct ward, sucked in a deep breath and blew it out again, and then pushed his way through. He didn't normally feel this way when visiting either suspects or victims, but this was different. This was personal.

Two nurses manned the reception desk. One was sitting at a computer while the other stood, flicking through paperwork of some kind. As he approached the desk, the nurse who was sitting glanced up. She was in her twenties, with dyed red hair tied back in a retro style with a headband, and she flashed him a smile.

"Hi there," she said. "You look a little lost."

"Do I?" His nervousness must have shown on his face. That wasn't good. "I think I'm in the right place." He flashed his ID, hoping it wasn't for long enough to allow her to get a good view of his name. "I heard Cole Fielding is awake. I wanted to have a word with him, if he's up for it."

Cole had been released from prison some time ago after serving his ridiculously short sentence for killing Hayley and he wondered how much the nurses knew of his past.

He hadn't told her why, hoping she'd make her own assumptions about that. If he said as little as possible, at least no one would be able to accuse him of lying.

She frowned. "He's awake, but he's not exactly in a condition to talk to you. He's managing some blinking in response to questions, but that's all."

Ryan's stomach knotted. He was blinking answers. Would that be enough to get the truth?

He tried not to let his feelings show on his face. "Anything might help at this point."

"It's impossible to know if he remembers anything that's happened to him."

So, she had assumed he was there to investigate the reason why Cole Fielding had ended up in a hospital bed for months on end.

"Is it likely that he'll get any better?" he asked.

"Honestly, we're all surprised he's made the improvements that he has. He's clearly a fighter, so anything is possible."

Anger roiled inside him at hearing the nurse speak of the man who killed Hayley as a 'fighter', and he forced himself to tamp it down.

Ryan kept his voice level. "Maybe finding out what happened to him will help."

Her eyes narrowed. "I thought he tried to kill himself."

"Yes, well, that's what we're assuming, but the investigation is ongoing, and of course, him being awake now changes things. He might be able to tell us differently."

She glanced around as though checking who was near and then hunched over a little and spoke in a low voice. "Okay, but don't stay too long. Ten minutes at the most, and if he starts getting distressed then you know it's time to leave."

"Of course."

That she didn't want Cole to be 'distressed' made him want to growl with fury. Distressed was the absolute least he deserved. Cole Fielding deserved to suffer, and yes, perhaps people would argue that he had, but even if he stayed like he was now—trapped inside his body with little way of communicating with the outside world—it still wouldn't feel like enough to Ryan. The sound of his mocking laughter in the courtroom would forever play in a loop in Ryan's head. Cole didn't deserve to have a life of any kind.

Ryan would always have said he was against the death penalty—and he'd even argue that he still was—but it was different when things were personal. Having to exist in a world with Cole Fielding still in it and Hayley wasn't, was the hardest thing to comprehend.

He ducked his head in a nod and made his way to the part of the ward containing the hospital beds and their patients.

God, what a depressing place to work. All these bodies lying in bed, mostly unresponsive. How could the doctors, and especially the nurses, stand to be around this all day, every day? How much could they even help their patients? They could feed them and keep them clean and turn them to prevent them getting bedsores, but the chance of them ever getting any better was slim to none. To care for a person who didn't even know what was happening around them and to get no thanks for it must be soul-destroying. Perhaps they would argue that their patients *were* aware of what was going on and they could hear everything that was being said, but there was still no proof of that.

Would Cole know he was there? He would if he was awake.

He headed to the final bed in the row. A couple of nurses worked with the other patients and offered him smiles and nods as he passed. Ryan knew his appearance helped put them at ease. Tall, not bad-looking, well-put-together in his suit. He had a smile he reserved for winning people over. It helped to be the kind of person others were open and receptive to, even though he felt as though he wore his persona as a mask to hide the neurotic mess he felt like he really was beneath.

Cole Fielding lay under a white hospital sheet, standard hospital wear covering his body. Ryan remembered the swaggering, cocksure man Cole had been in the courtroom. He'd worn his youth in that way young people did—as though it was a right and would last forever, and made him invincible. Now that man lying in the hospital bed appeared to be at least a decade older, his cheeks hollowed and his eye sockets two pits of shadows. His eyes were closed.

Ryan's heart beat faster, adrenaline flooding through him, heightening every sense. The stink of the hospital, all these bodies stagnant in bed. His breathing grew faster, but he forced himself to slow it. He'd been in plenty of difficult situations in his life and managed to keep his cool, but this felt different.

He stood over the bed. "Cole? Cole Fielding?"

Cole's eyes fluttered open. They were glazed and unfocused.

"I'm a detective, Cole. I wondered if I could ask you a couple of questions." Ryan held his breath, waiting for a response.

Would Cole recognise him? And if he did, would Ryan know if it was from the courtroom or from the night of Cole's accident, the same one that had landed him in this hospital bed?

Cole's gaze flicked in Ryan's direction and paused on him briefly before sliding past and focusing on something over Ryan's left shoulder.

Ryan tried again. "Cole? Do you know what happened to you the night of your accident? Can you blink once for yes and twice for no?"

He stared intently at Cole's ravaged face, checking for a response. If Cole had heard him, or understood him, he wasn't showing any sign.

He tried again. "Can you remember what happened to you? The reason why you're in hospital now. Blink once for yes, twice for no."

Cole might be awake in that he was breathing on his own and his eyes were moving, but how much of the person he'd once been was still in there? Did he have normal thoughts but was unable to make his body work well enough to convey them?

The heart monitor suddenly let out a shrill beep. Cole moaned then thrashed from side to side. His shoulders jerked, and his hips lifted from the bed. His eyes rolled back, showing the whites.

Ryan stepped back in shock. A nurse rushed up and checked the drip in Cole's arm and switched off the alarm. She put her hands on Cole's shoulders, pinning him down, and spoke to Ryan over her shoulder.

"It's time for you to go now."

Ryan wasn't going to argue. He turned and walked briskly from the ward before anyone else could ask who he was or what he was doing there. It wasn't as though he meant Cole any harm. Despite everything he thought about the man who'd killed his daughter, he hadn't come here to finish off the job. He wasn't a murderer, no matter what his intrusive thoughts insisted. The only time he'd ever even consider taking another life was if he had to bring down a criminal in order to save others.

He wouldn't have tried to kill Cole Fielding. He was positive.

Almost.

Chapter Twenty-Four

"I have an update on the Ford Transits that were seen around the area at that time."

Ryan had barely got in the office door before he was accosted by DC Penn.

"Tell me." Ryan shrugged off his jacket and hung it over the back of his chair.

"As you know, there were four vans fitting the description caught on CCTV from around the area between the hours of three and six a.m. on the Monday morning," Craig said. "Three are registered to businesses, and the other is privately owned. One of the vans belongs to a fruit and vegetable wholesaler, Seasonal Produce, based on Cheltenham Road. It was driven by fifty-three-year-old Barry Hayle. He was out on deliveries to all the shops that stock their produce and was able to produce a list of each of the places he visited between the hours of eleven p.m. and six a.m. the following morning, when his shift ended."

Ryan frowned. "Why do the deliveries in the middle of the night?"

"Less traffic on the roads. They can be done in a fraction of the time it would take during rush hour."

That made sense.

"Okay, we can rule him out then. Who's next?"

"The second belongs to a pet transporter who was bringing rescued dogs over from Spain. They had a drop-off several streets away from the Wyndhams' road."

"At three o'clock in the morning?" he checked.

Craig nodded. "Yes, they cover most of the country, driving several hours between places, dropping the animals off to their new homes. Two people were in the van; forty-year-old Mick Fraser and his wife, Annabel. They can prove that they were in Oxford before the murders, doing another drop-off, and then after the drop-off in Bristol, they drove straight down to Plymouth."

"Okay, so they wouldn't have had time to commit the murders."

"The vehicle privately registered belongs to a painter-decorator, Mark Ledlow. He's twenty-eight years old and lives with a flatmate in Bristol, who can attest to his whereabouts before he left that morning. He was driving to Bristol airport to catch an early flight to see family in Portugal. I've checked out his story, and it all fits. He's in Portugal now, actually."

"Lucky him."

Craig grinned. "I thought the same."

"And the fourth van?" Ryan prompted.

"Registered to a photography company. The director is Philip Sweeny, aged thirty-two. His most recent address is here in Bristol, but attempts to track him down have so far been unsuccessful, so we haven't been able to rule him out."

"That sounds promising. What else can you tell me about him?"

"The first thing I did was run a background check on him, and we already have him in our system. He was charged and convicted of ABH at the age of eighteen towards a foster parent, Mr Willis. Sweeny had aged out of foster care at that point but returned to the family home and attacked Mr Willis. He didn't serve any time but was put on a suspended sentence."

"Do we know why he attacked his foster father?" Ryan asked.

"It simply says a 'disagreement' on the file."

Ryan tapped his fingers against his lips. Was it worth sending someone out to interview the foster father, assuming he was still alive? At this point, they didn't know if Sweeny even had anything to do with the Wyndham murders.

"What kind of work does his photography company do?"

"He mostly seemed to work in residential properties for sale or rent."

Ryan frowned, not quite understanding. "He puts places on the market?"

"No, he doesn't. He works for estate agents who employ him freelance to go in and take photographs and also videos for these online virtual tours of properties for their websites."

Ryan remembered something Elouise had said, and his pulse quickened. "And the Wyndhams had put the place on the market because they'd been planning on emigrating to Australia. That must be our link."

Craig nodded. "Sounds like it could be."

"We need to find out which estate agents the Wyndhams had the property on with."

"I can find out," Craig offered.

"Make it a priority. Have you got an address for Sweeny?"

"Yes, here you go."

He slid a piece of paper onto Ryan's desk. "Also, I sent you a link. It's for Sweeny's website. Take a look."

Ryan opened his computer. Every muscle in his body was tense, priming himself for what he might find. He consciously loosened his jaw, aware it was clenched so tight he'd probably impact his molars. What sort of thing would Sweeny have online? He imagined a website like *Watch People Die*, which had been taken offline due to its increasingly graphic content, including an eighteen-year-old committing suicide, but when he clicked on the link Craig had sent, something completely different came up.

It was a professional photography website for a business called Property Studio. The header encouraged the viewer to take their property listings to a new dimension. A number of photographs of smart, modern buildings were on the front page.

Ryan clicked on one of the photographs and was surprised when it moved. So, this was what was meant by virtual tours. He could move his mouse and swing the view on his screen right the way around the room, and then if he pulled his mouse down, the view lifted to the ceiling, and if he dragged it up, he was able to see right down to the floor.

The footage allowed him to take a tour of this property right from stepping inside the front door, all the way through the house. He could count how many shoes were on the shoe rack, the exact number of stairs up the first floor, and see where the keys were left on the hall console. He could see the photographs of the family on the wall, and when he clicked to go into the kitchen, he was able to read the bills that had been attached to a cork pinboard on the wall.

"Jesus Christ."

This footage gave whoever had access to it an unfettered access to the exact layout of the house and the people who lived within it. It let him see exactly what locks were on every door and window, and where the keys were kept for each one.

His mouth ran dry, his heart beating harder. He had little doubt that this man had used this footage to learn everything there was to know about the Wyndhams and their home. His inside knowledge had allowed him to sneak in and out of the house. Maybe it had started with him just watching the videos to get a taste of their family life, but then when that hadn't been enough, he must have wanted more and started entering the home for real. He'd hidden himself inside the loft space, coming down at night or when the family were out.

A thought occurred to him. That was how he knew the bedroom windows had small keys sticking out of each of the locks. That he could lock the windows from the inside and remove the key and there was no way for either of the children to open a window and either climb out or shout for help. But how did he know the alarm code?

"Impressive, right?" Craig said, raising both eyebrows.

"This definitely wasn't what I'd been expecting."

"You think he used the videos he took of the Wyndhams' house to learn how to get around the place unseen?"

"It's definitely a possibility. Until we find him, and can ask him some questions, there's still the chance this is just a coincidence. Liz Wyndham complained about a white Transit van being outside of her house, but that doesn't mean whoever was driving it killed the family for sure. At this point, we don't have any actual evidence that Philip Sweeny was responsible. If he worked in this area anyway, he might have just been out on a job."

"At half past three in the morning?"

"Or someone else was driving the van. We don't know how many people he has working for him, or if he lends the vehicle to someone else?" Ryan lifted both hands in a helpless shrug. "I understand what you're saying, and this is excellent progress, but until we've got that physical proof, or can find the man himself to confess, we can't bring charges. We've still got a lot of work to do."

With this new development, Ryan needed to call a briefing.

He gathered his team together in the briefing room and ran them through the most recent findings, including the discoveries in the loft and what DC Penn had learned about the Ford Transits.

"Currently," he said, addressing the room, "Philip Sweeny is our biggest lead. He was known to us, with a prior conviction for violence against his foster father, but whether that means he also has it in him to murder a whole family in cold blood, I'm not yet sure. We believe he may have photographed the Wyndham house when they put it on the market briefly earlier this year. Craig is going to track down which estate agents they had it on with, but our main priority needs to be tracking down Sweeny." He looked to another of his DCs. "Linda, can you find out everything there is to know about him. Did he have any connection to the Wyndhams before they'd put it on the market? Any friends or relatives? Sweeny is a good decade younger than the Wyndhams, but I still want to know what schools they went to, or if they had any similar interests. I want to know what motive Sweeny might have for wanting the family dead."

Linda jotted down what he'd said.

"Does there always need to be motive?" Mallory said. "Some people just kill for the sake of killing."

He struggled to look at her with her eye all swollen half shut. "You're right, but if there is a motive, I want to know about it. We also need to track down Sweeny's van. If we find the vehicle, we might find him. Shonda, can I put you onto that?"

Shonda nodded. "You got it, boss."

"We know Sweeny has a business mobile phone as his number is on his website, but he could have a personal one as well. Dev, can you see if we can find out what network he's on and then get his records pulled."

"No problem, boss," DC Dev Kharral said.

Ryan continued. "I'm going to take DS Lawson and go to his flat, see what we can find out, and ask around the neighbours and find out what they know. Remember, right now, it could just be a coincidence that we spotted a similar van to the one Liz Wyndham had reported and we can't track down the person most likely to be driving. For all we know, Philip Sweeny is innocently on holiday and has no idea we're trying to track him down, and someone else was driving the van, but then again, he could be in hiding because he murdered the Wyndham family in their beds."

He took in the faces of his team who were all nodding in agreement.

"Let's get to it. I want Sweeny found by the end of the day."

RYAN PULLED THE CAR up outside the address they had registered for Philip Sweeny.

The flat where Sweeny lived was nothing like the sort of premises he'd expected. Where the photography website was all stately homes and posh apartments, his flat was in a rough area, with dirty windows and peeling paint around the frames.

Ryan climbed out of the car, and Mallory followed. He stopped and cupped his hands to the side of his face to peer through a window. Through the dirty glass, he could make out a living room, with a dilapidated orange sofa and an old television in the corner.

There was no sign of Sweeny.

He left the window and went to the door. The lower flat had a bell beside the number, and Ryan pressed his finger on the button. From inside the property came the muffled chime of a doorbell. Ryan gave Sweeny a moment to answer, and when there was no response, he pressed it again.

He lifted his fist and hammered on the door. "Police, Mr Sweeny. If you're in there, you need to open up."

"He's either not in," Mallory said, "or he's hiding out."

Ryan turned to her, chewing his lower lip. "We don't have enough on him to force entry, but we might have to start thinking about getting a warrant. Let's talk to some of the neighbours."

He rang the bell for the upstairs flat.

From above, a female voice called out of a window, "Can I help you?"

Ryan stepped back and held up his ID for the woman to see. She appeared to be in her seventies, with short hair dyed unnaturally black. "We're after Philip Sweeny. We'd like to have a quick word."

"Give me one minute."

He and Mallory exchanged a glance, and they waited for the woman to come down.

Thirty seconds passed, and the door opened, revealing the woman who was barely five feet tall and must only weigh seven stone.

"What do you want with Philip"? she asked.

"We need to talk to him regarding a case we're working on." Ryan had no intention of giving her any details. He didn't need for this to get out to the press and for them to start declaring they had a suspect. Doing so might give Sweeny a warning they were onto him. "When was the last time you saw Mr Sweeny?"

"Oh, gosh. It's been a while now. Almost a week."

"Can you think back to exactly when that was?"

Her already wrinkled brow furrowed further. "Hmm, I think it was after I'd come back from my Pilates class which is on a Friday evening. We start at seven, and I'm home by about quarter past eight."

"And you saw him then? What was he doing?"

"Looked like he was off out somewhere. He had one of those shoulder bags, you know the kind, like he was off to the gym."

"And this would have been around eight-fifteen?" Ryan checked.

"Yes."

"Was he on foot or driving a vehicle?"

"He has a white van that he always has parked around here. He got into that and drove off."

"Do you know where he was going?"

"I have no idea, sorry. We say hello to each other out of politeness's sake, since we're neighbours, but we don't have any real conversations." She gave a quick smile. "I mean, what would a young man want to say to someone like me anyway."

Ryan thought of his own neighbour and what good company she could be. "I'm sure you have plenty to say, Mrs...?"

He left the gap open for her to fill in.

"Rollick. Glenda Rollick. Is Philip in some kind of trouble?"

"I'm afraid I'm not at liberty to say."

She winked and tapped her finger against the side of her nose. "Top secret, eh? Don't worry, I won't tell him you were asking after him."

If they ended up forcing entry in to his flat, Ryan thought there was a good chance he might figure it out for himself, but he didn't say that to her.

"Does Philip live alone?"

"Yes, he does."

"What about friends or family? Does he ever have anyone with him?"

"No, I've never seen him with anyone else. He's always struck me as rather a lonely soul. I must say the same about myself, though. It's not easy being on your own. That's why I do all my classes, even at my age. Helps keep me connected to others, and keeps me fit as well, of course. Just 'cause you're older doesn't mean you should start letting everything go."

She had the chattiness he often saw in people who lived alone. It was as though they stored up their lack of conversation from living by themselves and regurgitated it all onto whoever was willing to listen.

"Thank you for your help. We'll let you get on with your day." He handed her a card. "If he does reappear, though, I'd appreciate a call."

"Of course, Detective."

She shut the door, and he and Mallory took a few steps down the street to distance themselves from the property.

"We need to interview each of the neighbours," he said, "find out if any of them know Sweeny and if they have any idea where he might be. We need to find that van, too. It has to be somewhere and if it was always parked around here, it doesn't look like anyone else would be driving it."

Ryan's phone rang, and he pulled it out of his pocket. The screen showed 'Maggie Bryant' who was part of the specialist fingerprint team, and so he answered it.

"Maggie, how's it going?"

"I've just sent you an email," she said down the line, "but I thought I'd better call you, too. You're going to be happy with the findings."

Chapter Twenty-Five

"Tell me," Ryan said.

"We were able to match them to prints on the system. They belonged to a Mr Philip Sweeny."

Ryan barely held back from punching the air. "Philip Sweeny is our man then. We're currently at his flat as a Ford Transit registered to his business was caught on CCTV on the morning of the murders." He sensed Mallory watching him intently and he nodded at her and mouthed, *it's him.*

"Excellent. Glad to have helped."

"Thanks for letting me know," her told Maggie. Ryan ended the call and turned to Mallory. "That definitely gives us enough evidence to get a search warrant for his flat."

"So, Sweeny is our guy?" Mallory asked.

"I'd say so. Everything is pointing to him. We just need to find out where he is."

She pulled a face. "Easier said than done. What is it with these men going missing right when we need to talk to them?"

"If they could just learn to walk right into the police station when we need them, it would make our job a lot simpler," he teased her. They both knew that was never going to happen. "We need to petition the magistrates' court for a search warrant. Make sure they know it's urgent."

Mallory nodded and took out her phone. "I'll get onto that right away."

He called for backup. "I need someone positioned outside the address of a suspect while we're waiting for a search warrant."

"You go," he told Mallory. "I'll wait here until the squad car turns up. I'm not going to risk Sweeny coming back and us missing him, or, if he's already in there, but is hoping we'll just go away, for him to do a runner."

"No problem, boss. I'll see you back in the office."

"With the warrant," he told her.

"Absolutely."

He watched her climb into the car and drive off, and then leaned against the wall of Philip Sweeny's flat to wait for backup. A steely determination settled inside him. Sweeny was their man, and Ryan wouldn't rest until he'd tracked him down. He remembered how he'd promised to keep Nikki Francis updated with progress. This was surely news worthy of a call? Or was he just using it as an excuse?

He took out his phone and scrolled to her number. She'd probably be busy. This might be better coming as an email. No, he dismissed the thought instantly. If he sent her an email, she'd probably string him up by his balls the next time she saw him.

He cleared his throat, hesitated once more, and then hit the call button. The phone rang, and he couldn't decide if he wanted her to answer or not, but then she did.

"Ryan," her warm voice came down the line. "To what do I owe the pleasure?"

"Hi, Nikki. I promised I'd keep you updated on the Wyndham case."

He hoped she wasn't going to be disappointed that he was calling for business reasons, but then he gave himself a mental slap. She was a beautiful, intelligent, professional woman. It wasn't as though he was exactly a catch. He had more baggage than the belly of an airplane.

"How's it going?"

"We have a name. A Mr Philip Sweeny. We've found his DNA at the scene, and a van licensed to his business was caught on CCTV the night of the murders. Looks like he may have taken videos and photos of the Wyndham house when they put it on the market."

"Oh my God. Why did he kill them?"

Ryan shrugged, even though she couldn't see him. "That's still something we're trying to work out."

"Well, I'm glad you've made progress."

"Me, too, though we still have to track him down."

"I'm sure you will. How have you been otherwise?" she asked.

"You know, the usual."

"Don't tell me," she said. "Busy?"

He could hear the smile in her voice and was glad she wasn't angry with him. "Yeah, still busy." He caught sight of the blue, yellow, and white of a response vehicle heading down the road towards him. "Speaking of busy, I've got to go. Uniform have just turned up."

"No problem. Thanks for calling, Ryan."

He was about to hang up and then stopped himself. "Oh, and Nikki, if you're ever thinking of putting your house on the market, don't let them do one of those online video tours."

"Got it," she said and ended the call.

He waved to flag down the driver of the response car. He'd leave an officer here and get the other one to give him a ride back to the office.

Two police officers climbed out, and Ryan gave them a rundown of where they were. It was agreed that one would stay guarding the flat until the search warrant came through. Ryan hoped it wouldn't take too long.

He got a lift back to the office, but before he could get in the door, he was accosted by DC Penn.

"Boss, I've tracked down the estate agents the Wyndham house was on with."

"Tell me," Ryan said.

"The property was marketed by Parks and Walker Estate Agents. They have their premises on Cathedral Walk. It was on the market for a whole ten days."

Ryan checked his watch. It was heading into late afternoon now, but they should still be open. "Let's pay them a visit, see what they know about Sweeny."

THE ESTATE AGENT WAS located in a modern building not far from the quay. The glass-fronted entrance was filled with current properties on the market—everything from huge townhouses worth millions, to properties with several acres out in the countryside. In the window on the right were the more 'normal' properties—terraced Bristol houses that were in the few hundred thousand price mark rather than several million. Even so, it was hard for people to get on the housing market with Bristol house prices what they were, and they seemed to be climbing all the time. He'd been lucky in that he'd bought before prices had gone crazy. Of course, then his marriage had broken down and he'd bought his overpriced flat. He hadn't wanted to rent. The idea of living somewhere that another person owned didn't sit right with him. He'd rather own a tiny, one-bedroom flat than live in a three-bedroom house where a landlord could tell him what pictures he was allowed to hang and could potentially kick him out with just a month's notice. He appreciated that he was lucky to have the option. Most of the younger generation had no choice but to rent.

He wasn't there to muse over the state of the housing market.

They entered the estate agents. A couple of smartly dressed women sat behind individual desks, and they both glanced up at Ryan and Craig, probably mistaking them for potential clients rather than police.

"Hi there," chirped the older of the two women. "How can I help?"

Ryan took out his ID, and her smile faltered.

"I'm DI Chase. I have some questions regarding a case. Can I speak to whoever is in charge here?"

"That would be me." She got to her feet and held out her hand to Ryan. "I'm Emma Fenn, and I'm the manager."

"Do you have a private office we could talk in?"

"Of course." She addressed her colleague. "You going to be all right without me, Becky?"

It wasn't as though they had anyone else in the office, but Ryan guessed the phones could get busy.

"Yeah, fine," the other woman said, flashing a curious but concerned smile.

Emma gestured to a door at the back. "Right this way."

She led them though into a small but tidy staffroom, containing a kettle and a microwave and an under-the-counter fridge. There were also a couple of two-seater sofas, and Emma nodded to one of them before taking a seat on the other.

Ryan perched on the edge of the sofa she'd nodded to, and Craig sat beside him.

"I wondered if you could remember marketing a property about five months ago. It was number forty-two Denville Road in Bedminster, owned by Liz and Hugh Wyndham."

Emma frowned. "That name does sound familiar. We've had an awful lot of houses put on the market between now and then, though. Were they on the market for long?"

"No, only a couple of weeks."

"They sold that fast?" She seemed surprised.

"No, they took the house off the market again."

She bit her lower lip. "I'm going to need to look it up, I'm afraid. I don't remember them off the top of my head."

"When they put the house on the market, they had photographs taken which included a virtual tour."

She nodded. "Yes, we try to do that with as many properties as possible now, though we do charge an additional percent on our cut to cover costs. Some people don't go for it, even though it increases the chance of a sale. A lot of people buy from all over the country and can't always visit a property in person, so having a virtual tour they can do online helps. It allows potential buyers to be able to feel like they're right inside the house."

"Can you give me the name of the person who takes the footage?"

"We have a few different people we use. They work independently, and we bring them in when we need them, but obviously they're not always available, so we have others as backups."

"Are you able to search up the name of the person who worked on the Wyndham house as well?"

"Sure, I can do that. Just give me a minute." She took out her phone and swiped the screen, frowning down at it.

Ryan was already fairly sure it was going to be Philip Sweeny, but in his time in his job, he'd learned never to take anything for granted. He'd been surprised at developments of a case more times than he could count.

"Yes, here it is. I do remember—" Her mouth rounded in an 'O' of surprise. "Oh my God. Now I know why I recognised that name. That's the poor family who was murdered a few days ago, wasn't it? They were killed in that house?"

There was little point in denying it. "Yes, that's them."

Her shock morphed to confusion. "And you think their murders had something to do with their house being on the market?"

"It's just a line of enquiry we're following up."

He could see her putting pieces of the questions he'd been asking together in her mind.

Her eyes widened. "You think whoever took video footage of their house might have had something to do with their deaths?"

"As I said, it's not something I can discuss. Can you tell me who worked on the house?"

"Umm, it was done by Property Studio, which means Philip Sweeny would have come out to take the photographs and video footage. He does a lot of work for us. He's always in and out of the office."

"When you say 'always in and out of the office', are you talking daily? Or longer between visits than that?"

"Sorry, more like weekly. But he does work for us on a regular basis."

"How many properties would you say he's worked on?"

She shrugged. "I really couldn't say. A lot. Probably a few a month. But he doesn't only work for us. Like I said, he's freelance, so I imagine he's working for a number of other estate agents in the city as well."

Ryan exchanged a glance with Craig. His colleague would be thinking the same. If Sweeny was working for lots of different places, it was going to make it harder to track him down.

"After Sweeny has given you the footage of the houses," Ryan asked, "is he then required to delete it?"

"Well, no. Technically, he owns the copyright on the video footage. It's in our contract when we sign up with a new client. I believe he likes to be able to use it for his own website, to bring in new customers for himself."

"Then he could go back and rewatch that footage as often as he likes. Get to know every detail there is to know about a person's house."

She blinked. "I-I guess so, yes."

Ryan had another question. "As an estate agent, do you ever take down passcodes for a client's alarm, if they're on your books."

She nodded. "Of course, and we'll have a set of keys as well, in case we have to do viewings when the homeowners aren't there. To be honest, I prefer to do viewings when the house is empty. I can get a better idea about what the potential buyer is thinking if they're not worried about offending the sellers."

"Could Sweeny have got hold of keys or an alarm code? Is he ever left alone in the office?"

She shifted awkwardly in her seat. "I mean, he's not here on his own completely. One of us is always going to be somewhere in the building. But yes, I suppose that is possible."

"I'm going to need to know the exact last time Sweeny was in the office and what house he worked on."

"I can find that out for you." She hesitated and said, "You don't think he had something to do with the murders, do you? He always seemed like a perfectly nice man. A little quiet, perhaps, but always polite."

Ryan didn't respond to the question. "If you could just look that up for me, I'd appreciate it."

She nodded and went back to her phone. "Right, it seems he did a job for us last month."

"Can you give me the details of the house he worked on? On second thoughts, can you give me the addresses of all the properties he's worked on over the past six months?"

"I'll print them out." She gestured at the door. "The printer's out in the office."

Ryan rose to his feet and straightened out the front of his suit trousers. "We'll come with you. I think we have everything we need for now, but we may be in touch at a later time."

They filed back out into the office. The other estate agent, Becky, was sitting with a couple now, going over property details. Everyone glanced over with awkward smiles as they made an appearance.

Emma went over to the printer and retrieved the details. She handed them to Ryan.

He glanced down at them. It contained a list of at least fifteen different properties.

"Thanks for this," he said. "Here's my card. If you see Philip Sweeny, don't mention that we want to talk to him, just pick up the phone and call me. Okay?"

"Okay."

"Thank you for your time."

He and Craig left the building and stepped back out onto the street.

"That must be how he's picked his victims," Craig said. "But does it help us track him down?"

Ryan blew out a breath and held up the property details. "We'll check on these people, but if he worked for multiple estate agents, he could have covered numerous other houses before or after this one."

He was going to need to get more people onto this. There were a lot of estate agents in the city, and they needed to contact every single one.

Chapter Twenty-Six

Ryan got back in the office and called a briefing. DCI Hirst attended as well, sitting at the back of the room.

"I appreciate it's getting late, everyone, but we can't take our foot off the gas just yet."

He'd printed off a photograph of Philip Sweeny which he'd then attached to the board on the wall. Ryan had taken it from Sweeny's photography site. The man looked completely harmless. He had one of those faces that was neither handsome nor ugly. Easily forgettable. He was smartly dressed in a shirt but had forgone the tie, creating a smart but relaxed persona. Who'd have thought he'd have it in him to murder a whole family in their beds.

"We're ninety-nine percent sure this is the perpetrator of the Wyndham murders. Philip Sweeny is thirty-two years old, unmarried, with a current address here in Bristol. He was last seen by his neighbour, Glenda Rollick, on Friday evening at eight-fifteen, leaving his house carrying a duffle bag. She doesn't think he's been back since. What did he have in that bag? Clothes he changed into after he'd slaughtered the Wyndham family? The murder weapon, maybe? Was he on his way to the Wyndham house to hide in their loft or did he go somewhere else before then? Figuring out his movements might help us locate him now." Ryan took a breath. "We've put in for a search warrant for his flat, which I'm hoping will come back soon, and once we're able to conduct the search, we may get some idea of where he is."

Ryan pointed to another picture—that of the security footage of the Ford Transit. "As well as Sweeny, his van is also missing. If we can find the van, I suspect Sweeny won't be too far away. We've put out an attention drawn call, so hopefully it'll get spotted soon. There's a good chance Sweeny is just hiding out. Perhaps he realises we're onto him and so he's made himself scarce. However, as much as I hate saying it, there's also a chance Sweeny is in the process of picking his next victims. We need to contact every estate agent in the city and find out which of them have worked with Philip Sweeny."

"How many estate agents are in Bristol?" DC Dev Kharral asked. "It must be a lot."

Ryan nodded. "A quick search says there's almost two hundred, but some of those estate agents were the same company just with multiple offices. From there, we need to find out which of those estate agents had employed Sweeny to do virtual tours. Even with Sweeny only working on one property a day over the past six months, we're still looking at over a hundred potential properties, and so over a hundred potential victims."

"We could just check their websites," Linda suggested. "We could only talk to those who have the virtual tours featured."

"No, it's not enough. Someone might have employed him to take videos but not uploaded them yet."

She conceded. "Good point."

"This is going to take some old-fashioned legwork. Divide the city up between you, and contact each of the estate agents, find out if they worked with Sweeny, then get the listings from the last six months that he worked on."

Ryan looked to Dev. "How did we get on with getting his phone records?"

"No luck, sorry, boss. Can't find any personal number registered in his name, and the work phone has been switched off so we can't trace it. The records came back, but nothing on there is showing anything unusual. I've been able to match the calls to a number of estate agents, so we can probably use the numbers to help us figure out who he's worked with recently."

"Okay. Have we found any relatives of Sweeny's? Perhaps someone he might have gone to?" He focused his attention on Linda Quinn who he'd tasked with that action.

Linda's lips had thinned. "I went to speak to Sweeny's old foster parent, Mr Martin Willis. If you remember, Sweeny was charged and convicted of ABH when he was eighteen after attacking Mr Willis?"

Ryan nodded to show he remembered.

She continued. "Mr Willis had an interesting story. He says Philip Sweeny was always a troubled boy, and that it didn't surprise him that things ended how they had. Sweeny was put into the system at the age of seven after he was taken from his mother who was a drug addict. She went on a five-day binge in London and left him to fend for himself. The neighbours called the police after they caught him going through their bins for food."

Ryan shook his head. "Jesus Christ."

"It gets worse. Before he came to the Willis house, he was in a different family home where he attacked the eleven-year-old son of the family, trying to cut the boy's ear off with a kitchen knife. Luckily, he failed. When he was asked why he did it, he said the other boy was always getting all the attention. The family didn't press charges. I guess they were just happy to have him gone."

"My God."

"After that, he spent some time back in a group home and then was fostered out to a family whose children were already grown and had left home—the Willises. Things went well enough, but then after he'd aged out, he found out the foster parents were separating, and he attacked the father, Mr Willis, who was the one to leave."

"So, he has some serious dysfunction around families."

"Certainly seems that way."

"But why does he do it?" Ryan mused. "Why go and hole himself up at someone else's house? "

"Maybe he feels he wants to be part of a family?" Linda suggested.

"A family he ends up murdering because he feels like they've somehow let him down again?"

Ryan turned to the board containing the names and photographs of everyone who'd been of interest so far. His gaze alighted on the image of Elouise Lewis. "Maybe he found out about the babysitter. Perhaps that shattered his idea of a perfect family life, and he couldn't handle it, so he killed them all."

He let the idea simmer with his team and then moved on.

"What about more recently? With that kind of background, how did he end up becoming a photographer?

Linda continued. "From what I can tell, he always did well at school. After the attack on Mr Willis, to all intents and purposes, he got his life back on track."

"Did he ever marry? Have kids?"

"Not that I can tell. He lives alone now. Maybe that's why he's felt the need to stalk these families. I don't know...perhaps his job set him off. Maybe he was doing all these video shoots for the agencies and seeing these perfect homes and perfect families and perfect lives, and he wanted to be a part of it."

"Except when he got too close, he realised they weren't as perfect as he thought."

"And so he killed them all."

"And now he might be out there, planning to do the same to another family."

Linda shuddered. "I don't think I'll ever be able to put a house on the market again."

"Same. It certainly makes you think twice about the amount of access to your home that you're giving to complete strangers."

It had been some time since Ryan had sold a house, but he remembered the conversations he and Donna had had about putting their place on the market. Since Hayley had died when they'd decided to divorce, it wasn't as though either of them had any right to stay more than the other. The thought of them selling their family home had filled him with melancholy, however. It was supposed to have been the place they'd raise their family in, and instead it had been the final thing that had divided them. He'd been relieved in the end that Donna had wanted to stay there. Strangely, it made him feel as though he still had a home.

Ryan shook off the sadness. He had plenty of time to mope around after they'd caught this bastard.

A light knock came at the briefing room door, and Mallory stuck her head in and waved an A4 piece of paper with the magistrates' heading on it.

"Boss, we've got the warrant through to search the Sweeny flat."

"Let's get to work then, everybody," he instructed his team.

"We'll find him," DCI Hirst told him as he passed her leaving the briefing room. "The son of a bitch can't hide out forever."

He appreciated her faith in him and wished he could feel the same way about things himself.

He took out his phone to call for a Tactical Aid Unit to meet them at the property since they were search-trained officers. Time was of the essence. He couldn't shake the feeling that if he didn't find Sweeny soon, more innocent people were going to lose their lives.

BACKUP WAS ALREADY at Sweeny's flat when Ryan and Mallory arrived. The blue-and-white marked Tactical Aid Unit van was parked outside the property, and Tactical Aid officers climbed out of the vehicle to greet them.

"DI Chase," he introduced himself to them. "Thanks for coming. This is the property we need to gain access to."

If there had been any immediate risk to life, Ryan would have broken in there himself, but since he was certain Philip Sweeny had already taken up residence in his next victims' home, he'd needed to wait for the warrant.

"No problem," said the Police Search Advisor. "Happy to help."

They had a battering ram to break down the door, and Ryan stepped back to allow the officers to do their job.

The neighbours were all noticing something was going on now, emerging from their front doors, or peering through their front room windows to get a good view of the police activity.

Loud, repetitive thuds came from the front door as the biggest of the officers slammed the battering ram into Philip Sweeny's front door. It only took a couple of decent hits, and the door flew inwards, giving them access. A small pile of post was littered across the carpet.

Ryan stepped in behind the officers. "Wherever Sweeny is right now," he said, "I'd say he's not been home recently."

Mallory looked over at him. "Where is he then?"

"My fear is that he's already picked out his next victim and has holed himself up in their house somewhere." Ryan dreaded the thought of waking up tomorrow to learn the news another family had been slaughtered.

The search team had already made their way into the flat.

"We need anything that might give us an idea where he's gone," Ryan told them. "It could be his most recent job—so addresses, photographs, property details for a house. Also, anything that might link him to the Wyndham house."

In years gone by, Ryan might have expected to find actual photographs of people or places, but he thought that was going to be unlikely.

Ryan pulled on a set of gloves from his pocket. He had no idea what he expected or hoped to find inside the property. While he wanted definitive evidence that Sweeny was their man, and would leave the Crown Prosecution Service in no doubt that they should charge Sweeny with the murders of each of the Wyndham family murders, his gut instinct told him their main focus needed to be on finding out where he was now.

The place was musty, the air stale, as though no one had lived there for a long time, despite knowing otherwise. The sofa was up against one wall. A small boxy television sat on a glass stand. Everything was covered in a thin layer of dust.

"Where's all his equipment?" Ryan wondered out loud. "We know what he does for a living, but there's no sign of it here."

"He's taken it with him," Mallory said.

"He must have done."

A shout came from the direction of the bedroom. "Boss, you're going to want to see this."

Ryan and Mallory exchanged a glance and followed the sound of the shout. They entered the bedroom, and Ryan drew up short. Floor-to-ceiling bookshelves painted black covered the entire back wall, but they didn't contain books.

Instead, rows and rows of DVDs were stacked on the shelves.

Ryan approached and slid one of the DVDs out. They weren't of the usual blockbuster movies most people had but were blank DVD cases for copying files. On the DVD Ryan had pulled out was written: *21 Fore Street*. He put that DVD back and took out another one. *6 Driver Lane* was the title of the next. He knew without needing to look any further that each of the DVDs contained video footage of the houses Sweeny had worked on

"Jesus Christ, there must be hundreds here."

Mallory shook her head. "Why keep the DVDs? Isn't everything online these days?"

"Perhaps he felt too vulnerable online. Take the video, make a copy, send what was needed to the estate agents and delete it."

Could Sweeny be at one of these addresses now? It was going to take them forever to go through each of them.

"We're going to need to bag them all up," he told the search team.

He turned away, shaking his head. This was going to take them all night, but he couldn't do it all himself. He'd been at work since eight a.m., and at some point, they were all going to need to get some rest.

Chapter Twenty-Seven

It was the first night that Andy was staying down in Exeter for work.

Helen didn't like sleeping in an empty house. Not that it was empty, exactly—the kids were still here—but it didn't feel the same without having Andy lying next to her. She always complained about how he'd snore or steal the covers or wake her up when he got up to go to the toilet, but now he wasn't here, she missed him.

She tossed and turned, first getting too hot and throwing off the covers, and then getting too cold and pulling them back over her body.

What was Andy doing now? Was he asleep in bed or doing something else?

She was a trusting person, but that little niggle of doubt wormed its way into her head. He'd be meeting all these new people at his job, and some of them were bound to be young, pretty, and female. When he came home, all she did was snipe at him, and he was probably relieved to be able to go out for dinner and then retire to a plush white hotel bed.

Would he be alone when he did so?

She shook the thought from her head. Yes, of course he would. Andy wasn't like that. He'd never given her any reason to doubt him. But now the miles had quite literally put distance between them, and she was worried about things that had never bothered her before. She'd always known he wouldn't be having an affair 'cause he'd always been at home with her, watching TV and eating dinner, and going up to bed, but now he could be doing anything.

From somewhere in the house, a soft shuffle followed by a thud caught her attention. She listened for the familiar click of the bathroom light or a flush of the toilet, signalling one of the kids had got up to use the bathroom, but none followed.

She frowned. They'd better not still be up on their phones. She often got up during the night to see the faint glow from beneath their bedroom doors that betrayed them being on their devices way after bedtime.

Helen huffed out a breath and threw back the covers again. She planted both feet on the carpet and got to her feet. Her bedroom door was shut, her room dark, but she knew the house well enough to navigate the room without bumping into anything. She reached the door, found the handle, and opened it.

A crash came from somewhere nearby, and her heart lurched. A scream escaped her throat before she'd even thought to try to stop it, and she clamped her hand over her mouth.

Her daughter's bedroom door flung open. "Mum! What's going on?"

Helen could see that Reese was all right. Was it her son?

"Tyler?" she called. "Tyler, are you okay?"

She raced across the landing but came to a halt before she reached her son's room. His door was still shut, but between them were the stack of boxes. Only this time, instead of the boxes having shifted slightly to one side, they had completely fallen.

"Tyler!" she called again, annoyed. "Get out here."

The bedroom door finally opened, and Tyler emerged, blinking tiredly, his dark hair mussy. "Why are you shouting?"

"Don't give me that. Have you been out here messing around? You knocked the boxes down!"

"No, I didn't."

"Well, they didn't just fall over by themselves, and I saw your sister come out of her room seconds after it happened, so there's no way she knocked them over and got back to her room without me seeing her."

His jaw dropped. "Seriously, Mum. I didn't touch the boxes. I was sound asleep, and you just woke me up."

"Don't bullshit me, Tyler." She put out her hand. "Give me your phone."

"What? Why?"

"Because I assume you were up on your phone and that's why you knocked over the boxes. What were you doing? Wandering around, staring at your phone so you didn't see them or something?"

"No, I was asleep! I already told you." His voice rose with what he seemed to believe was the unfairness of it all.

"I'm not messing around, Ty. Do you have any idea how tired I am at the moment, trying to deal with you kids on my own every day, plus sort the house out for viewing? All I ask for is a little help and instead I have you messing around in the middle of the night. Now go and get your phone."

He opened his mouth to protest, but she cut him off.

"*Now*, Tyler."

He turned to go back into his room, muttering, "This is unbelievable." He returned a moment later, his phone in his hand. He shoved it at her, and she took it.

"Good, now go back to bed."

She shook her head at the boxes. She wasn't going to deal with it now. She turned to go back to bed, but Reese was still standing at her bedroom door.

"What?" Helen asked her.

"Do you really think it was Tyler, Mum? What if he's telling the truth and it wasn't him?"

"It was him. Who else could it be?"

"I thought I saw someone in the house the other night, remember?"

Helen's heart stuttered, and a flush of cold water seemed to go through her veins, chilling her from the inside. Her breath suddenly felt shallow, and she wished more than anything that Andy was with them.

"Stop it, Reese."

"What? I haven't done anything. I was just reminding you, that's all."

"I hadn't forgotten!" Her fear was making her snappish, and she was taking it out on the kids. She forced herself to take a deep breath. "You and your brother need to stop this. I know things are a bit strange right now with your dad not being here and knowing that we have to move away from Bristol, and it's probably normal that you're both acting out, but seriously, I don't know how much more I can take."

"Oh my God, this is not us 'acting out'. We're not toddlers, Mum. Why won't you just believe what we say? I *did* see someone the other night, and Tyler was asleep. You could tell that just by looking at him."

Helen raised a hand in a stop sign. "That's quite enough, Reese. I'm not having this conversation tonight. It's late, and we all have to get up in the morning."

"But, Mum, what if someone is in the house? What if they knocked down the boxes?"

"Oh, Jesus Christ."

She wasn't going to get a moment's peace until she'd been and checked the house. She had no doubt that they were alone in here...okay, maybe some doubt, but only the kind that came from it being the middle of the night and feeling slightly spooked. Like her daughter, she was dressed in an oversized t-shirt for bed. She decided it covered enough of her legs for her to go and search the house. It wasn't as though she was going to come face to face with anyone anyway. She was only doing this to keep Reese happy. She still had Tyler's phone in her hand, which gave her a little reassurance. If there was anything strange, she would call nine-nine-nine. Not that there was going to be anyone, she reminded herself.

Helen left Reese and started down the stairs.

"Mum, wait," her daughter called.

Reese hurried after her. "I'm not going to let you go down there on your own."

Helen smiled and squeezed her daughter's hand. She could be sweet sometimes.

Together, they crept down the rest of the stairs. Helen flicked on the lights for the entrance hall and then entered the living room and turned on that light as well. No one was in there, just as she'd expected. She checked behind the sofa and the curtain, to prove to Reese it was empty, and then they went through into the kitchen-diner.

She flicked on the lights. "See, no one here."

Reese pointed to the downstairs cloakroom. "What about in there?"

Helen rolled her eyes, feeling more like the teenager than her teenager. She turned on the light on the wall and opened the door. There was nowhere to hide in the small space.

"Happy now?"

"Not really." Reese pouted. "Maybe we're being haunted."

"Oh, for goodness' sake. How long have we been living in this house now? We are *not* haunted."

"The ghost might be angry we're moving out without them."

Helen found herself holding back a laugh. "You are joking now, right?"

Reese widened her eyes. "It *might* be!"

"Come on, back to bed. No more talk of ghosts or seeing strange people in the house. One thing we all need is some more sleep."

Reese let out a sigh. "Fine."

Helen checked the doors were locked and then switched off all the lights again. The two of them made their way back up the stairs.

"Night, sweetie," Helen told her daughter.

"Night."

Helen went into her bedroom and shut the door behind her. She got back into bed and pulled the covers up to her chin. Even though they'd checked the house and she'd said all the right things to her daughter to reassure her, Helen still felt uneasy. Her heart beat too hard and fast, and though it was the middle of the night, she was wide awake. Her ears strained for any unusual sounds in the house.

It was a long time before she managed to fall back asleep.

Chapter Twenty-Eight

Ryan got into work after only a few hours' sleep. There had been no progress overnight on finding Philip Sweeny. No one had seen him, and his Ford Transit hadn't been located either. Ryan assumed that meant the van was off the road somewhere, perhaps hidden in a garage, which made their job even harder.

The atmosphere in the office was tense. No one had got much sleep, and he knew his team was as frustrated about not having found Sweeny yet as he was. Everyone was tetchy and short with each other. He kept a special eye on Mallory. Her swollen eye had gone down, and she was able to cover the worst of the bruising with makeup now, but she still looked exhausted.

The search on Sweeny's flat had only given them more potential properties rather than helping them narrow things down. They'd removed five hundred and forty-six DVDs of different homes that Sweeny had videoed over the past ten years, including the DVD of the Wyndham house. The DVDs hadn't been in any order that they'd been able to work out, including the year they'd been shot, alphabetic order of addresses or names, or the distance apart the homes themselves were in real life. Ryan had hoped that perhaps Sweeny had organised them according to which house he was most interested in, but the Wyndham house DVD had been located in the middle of all the others, and they appeared to be random, giving Ryan nothing to go on.

A large part of his team was being used to go through each of the DVDs in turn in the hope one might tell them where Sweeny was now.

Craig approached his desk. "Boss, we've put a list together of all the properties we can find that Sweeny has worked on over the past six months. It's not good news. As you'd predicted, there are over a hundred, and that's across twelve different estate agents."

"Shit."

Ryan took a moment to think.

What were they going to do? Go to every house on the list and have each property searched? The scale of the job was huge, and, in the meantime, he was going to terrify every inhabitant of the city who'd recently put their house on the market. It would be a massive operation, and DCI Hirst wasn't going to like it either. It would take some serious manpower.

What other choices did they have? Maybe Sweeny hadn't known that Hugh wasn't Sheldon's real father when he'd started stalking them? Was that enough to push him off the edge?

"Let's try to narrow things down before we start searching every property on the list. Look at the houses with families similar to the Wyndhams—the classic two-point-four family, with two kids, a boy and a girl, and two parents."

Craig nodded. "Sounds sensible."

Ryan thought of something else. "And use the photographs taken at Sweeny's flat to check the order of the DVDs and compare them to the properties he's worked on recently. See if you can find a pattern. It might help us narrow them down. Bring whoever you need on board to get it done."

They needed all the help they could get.

Something else troubled Ryan. What if he was on completely the wrong track? Sweeny might not even be anywhere near one of the other houses. He could have left the country, for all they knew, or was hiding out at a friend's place—not that they'd been able to find out if Sweeny *had* any friends.

He had to trust his gut on this.

Chapter Twenty-Nine

Helen stood on the landing beneath the loft hatch and craned her neck to look up at it. The torch felt heavy in her hand. Maybe she should wait until the weekend when Andy was home and send him up there to do this? They'd lived in this house for eight years, but she could count the number of times she'd been up into the loft on one hand, and she didn't think she'd ever been up there without Andy going up first. Even the thought of opening the hatch and pulling down the ladder filled her with anticipation. What if a whole heap of giant black spiders fell on top of her? She'd scream so loudly the neighbours would hear.

Cold sweat prickled across her hairline.

She gave herself a shake. She was being ridiculous. She was a strong, independent woman and she didn't need a man in the house to be able to go into her own loft. She needed the boxes that were still up there from the last time they'd moved. They were broken down and flat, but she was sure she remembered them still being there. If she was going to break the back on this packing malarky, she had to get them.

What about the noises?

Helen pushed the thought from her head. The sounds she'd heard the previous night didn't mean anything. There were always strange noises coming from an old house, and she'd been moving stuff around recently, so she was bound to have put things on creaky floorboards and unsettled the status quo.

Maybe Reese was right about them being haunted.

A smile tweaked her lips. "Come on, you can do this."

She reached for the metal hook that was kept propped in the corner of the landing and lifted it into the air. It took a couple of attempts, but she managed to hook the end into the circle that operated the catch and knocked it to one side.

The hatch flapped open, and she spied the twin ends of the ladder. Still using the hook, she latched on to the first rung of the ladder and pulled it across and then down. It fell faster and heavier than she'd expected, and she dropped the hook to grab the metal rungs. With the feet firmly on the floor, she gave it a tug, making sure it was stable.

She blew out a breath.

It was so dark up there, full of cobwebs and spiders. She hated spiders, especially ones that would get caught in her hair and crawl down the back of her shirt. She shuddered at the thought.

Helen took hold of the side of the ladder with one hand. Her other hand was filled with the torch, but there was no way she was going to relinquish that. The thought of going up there in total darkness was an absolute no-no. Climbing a ladder one-handed wasn't ideal, but she didn't have much choice.

Taking it rung by rung, she climbed. It was awkward getting up with the torch in one hand, and she clung tight with her other one. She'd never been good with heights, even if it was just up a few rungs of a ladder. Her head entered the dark square of the hatch, and then her shoulders. She had to duck a beam as she half climbed, half crawled up into the loft.

Helen clambered up and then straightened as much as she dared. She swung the torch beam overhead, and, just as she had feared, the light illuminated swathes of thick white cobwebs hanging from the beams. Beyond the beams were the backs of the roof tiles, and beyond those was the endless sky.

Dragging her thoughts away from spiders, she moved the torch beam down and used it to light the floor—or what there was of it. Some boards had been nailed down, creating a walkway between the beams and the insulation. It seemed stable enough, but she still feared the thought of putting too much weight on it and ending up going through the ceiling.

This is why I don't like lofts.

She scanned around for the boxes. Considering how many years they'd been in the house, they'd managed not to accumulate too much stuff in the loft. There were a couple of old suitcases and a box or two of Christmas decorations, but that was it. The rest of the house had plenty of storage, so they'd used that rather than going through the faff of having to climb up here.

Where were those bloody boxes? Had they got rid of them at some point and she'd forgotten? Maybe they'd got damp and Andy had thrown out them without telling her.

A chimney breast ran up through the middle of the loft, and she finally saw the boxes, flattened down, as she'd expected, and propped up against the brickwork. They were bigger than she'd remembered, and she was going to need to throw each one down the hatch and hope they'd be in one piece when they hit the landing. There was no way she'd be able to climb back down the ladder carrying the boxes and the torch.

She ducked another beam and tried not to squeal as cobwebs danced against the back of her neck. God, she hated this place.

From behind the chimney breast came the sound of someone trying to stifle a cough.

Helen froze, her heart jackhammering against the inside of her ribs. Had she really heard that? She couldn't have. That was crazy. It must have come from outside and there were just some weird acoustics in here.

Yes, that was it. Weird acoustics. The loft was freaking her out. She needed to grab the boxes and get back down into the house.

She picked up the first of the boxes. The movement sent years of dust cascading into the air, motes filling the yellow light of the torch.

The same stifled cough came again.

She hadn't misheard that, had she?

Oh God. The movements she'd heard during the night, the things she'd blamed on Tyler. The person Reese had seen. Was there someone up here?

There was no way she was going to call out to see if she got an answer. She needed to get out of there and phone the police. Why had she left her phone downstairs? She should have brought it with her!

The light from the loft hatch looked like freedom, and she ran towards it, as fast as she dared across the uneven, unstable floor, while having to duck beams.

Pain seared through her scalp, and suddenly she was flying backwards, her feet in the air. Someone had hold of her ponytail and had used it to yank her back. She managed a scream, but only a second or so escaped her lips before a hand clamped over her mouth. In her shock, she dropped the torch, and it hit the floor. The light went out, plunging her into darkness, and somewhere in that dark the torch rolled out of reach.

Helen kicked out, her shoes striking the floorboards. She clutched at the hand across her mouth, trying to drag it back off, but whoever had her was too strong. She slapped and clawed, her thoughts a blind rush of panic.

The fingers of the hand moved up and pinched her nostrils, and a new kind of terror engulfed her. She couldn't breathe!

Oh God, oh God, oh God, oh God.

No matter how much she tried to whip her head from side to side, trying to dislodge him, nothing worked. Her lungs burned, somehow feeling as though they were both swelling and shrinking at the same time.

Breathe! She needed to breathe! Just a tiny gasp of air. She'd do anything for it. But he wasn't going to let her.

The strength went from her muscles, and her arms fell loosely to her sides. Her vision had already gone fuzzy, but she couldn't tell if that was from the lack of light in the loft or lack of oxygen to her brain.

Finally, now she'd stopped struggling, he released her and lowered her fully to the floor. She needed to signal to her lungs that she could breathe again now, but her body seemed beyond her control.

Feet and legs stepped past her, navigating the inside of the loft towards the hatch.

Helen was vaguely aware of the loft ladder being pulled back up. Then the hatch closed, shutting off the last of the light.

Chapter Thirty

Disappointed. That was his overriding emotion. How could people make out like things were so perfect when that was far from the truth? Lies. It was all lies. Posting photographs on social media with hashtags of *so blessed* when behind closed doors they barely spoke to one another.

The secrets. That was the worst of it. The creeping around and lies that spilled so easily off the tongue. Did they think people wouldn't notice? These things always caught up to you eventually.

For a while, he thought he'd found one, but then it had all changed. The more time he spent with them, the more quickly their perfect lives became unravelled. Then the anger started. They'd fooled him, had wasted his time. How was anyone supposed to live like this? So, he made the decision that they didn't get to live.

Now *she* had ruined things. Why did they *always* have to ruin things? She could have just stayed down there, where she belonged, and allowed him to be a part of their lives, but instead she had to come up to his domain and start poking around.

He'd so hoped this one was going to be different. While he knew he couldn't stay with them forever, it had felt good to be a part of things, to listen to normal family life happening around him. He didn't know how that felt—to be part of a normal family. The two-point-four children, and the loving mother and father. True, he'd been a bit disappointed when Andy had said he needed to work away from home a few days during the week, to stay in a hotel instead of being with his family, but *he* understood. It was what a good man did to take care of his wife and children—he made sacrifices. He was sure Andy would have preferred to be in bed next to his wife rather than in a cold, sterile hotel room.

He thought the last family were perfect, but he'd been so very wrong. It had been partly his fault. He hadn't realised that Hugh wasn't the boy's biological father—that had been his first mistake. Families that started with the baggage of marriages that had already been broken, of children who had already suffered at the hands of their parents, were already doomed. He should have known that. But then he'd overheard the arguments about the girl down the street, and he'd known then that this family had no chance. They weren't going to make it.

He'd saved them. They might not have seen it that way, but he had. He'd saved them years of heartache and resentment and anger.

He'd thought this one was going to be different. Maybe they would have been if only Helen had stayed put. Now he had to deal with her, and that would mean having to deal with the children as well.

It wasn't what he'd planned, but they'd left him with no choice.

Chapter Thirty-One

DC Shonda Dawson approached Ryan's desk. He could tell by the excited grin on her face, and the way she was practically bouncing on her toes, that she had something big to tell him.

"Boss, we've found the Ford Transit," she said. "It's partly hidden on a piece of scrubland in Lawrence Hill."

He didn't want to celebrate too soon. "It's definitely the right one?"

"It has the correct licence plate."

"Any sign of anyone in there?"

"No, and from the number of fallen leaves on the windscreen and roof, it doesn't look like it's been moved for a while."

"Good work. We're going to need a warrant to search it. Can I leave that with you?" He checked his watch. It was still mid-afternoon, so they had a couple of hours to get to the magistrates' court.

She nodded. "Absolutely. I'll go down right away. Hopefully SOCO will be able to lift something we can use from the vehicle."

"We already have forensics putting him at the Wyndham house, but a good defence lawyer could argue that the presence of fingerprints on a fork in the loft was down to him taking his lunch up there for some reason when he'd gone there to video the house. If we can find blood in the van, that will certainly help get a conviction. What we could really do with is finding a damn address book to give us an idea of where he's gone."

"If it's the right vehicle, can we assume that Sweeny might be somewhere nearby?"

"That's an excellent point. It's in Lawrence Hill, did you say?"

"That's right."

"Thanks, that gives us something to work with."

Shonda left for the magistrates' court, and Ryan called Mallory over. "We've found the van in the Lawrence Hill area. Let's run through all the properties Sweeny has worked on recently. How many of them are nearby?"

Mallory frowned. "What are we calling recently?"

He thought for a moment and then said, "Let's start within the last month and take it from there."

Together, they went through the list. There were only two houses listed in the Lawrence Hill area from the past month, but when they expanded to the following month, that became five houses, and then three months in there were eight.

Ryan sucked air in over his teeth. "We need to send officers out to each of these properties and check if everything's all right. Can you coordinate with uniform and cross-match what comes in to the addresses we've narrowed down. I want to hear about anything unusual that gets reported by anyone living in one of those addresses."

"Of course, but if Sweeny is hiding, will the residents of the houses even realise he's there?"

"We'll have to ask the people who live there if they're happy for us to search the premises."

She winced. "Not everyone is going to like that, and it's going to leave some of them feeling pretty shaken up at the idea that a murderer might be living in their home."

"I'd rather people were shaken up than dead," he said. "Honestly, Mallory, I hope I'm wrong about this. I hope he's fled the country on a fake passport and there isn't another family in danger right now, but I don't think that's what's happened."

Chapter Thirty-Two

"Mum, I'm home!"

Reese dropped her bag on the kitchen table and shrugged off her coat and draped it over the back of the chair. The house was strangely quiet. Her mum was normally home by now, making a big show of still being busy, despite having finished work. She'd be noisily emptying the dishwasher, doing it deliberately loudly as to make a point that no one else had done it.

What was that called? Passive-aggressive. But maybe her or her brother should at least attempt to empty it now Dad wasn't home in the week and their mum *was* actually having to do everything.

Where was her brother? Oh yeah, it was Friday, and he'd be at the afterschool football club. Maybe their mum had left early to go and pick him up, though she always complained that he was old enough to walk by himself now, which he probably was.

Reese fished out her phone from her bag and scrolled through to find her mother's number. She swiped 'call' and pressed it to her ear.

From somewhere in the house, her mum's phone rang.

Reese frowned and lowered her own phone. "Mum?" she called out again.

Maybe her mum was home then. She was as bad as the rest of them with their phone addictions and never left home without it. Yet Reese could hear it ringing. Maybe her mum wasn't feeling well and had gone to have a lie down.

Reese followed the ringing, but it didn't take her upstairs. Instead, she walked through into the living room to discover the phone left on the coffee table. Reese ended the call on her own phone and then stooped to pick up her mother's. She must have just forgotten it.

But something else niggled at her, something that wasn't quite right.

She turned around, trying to figure out what it was, and, as she did so, caught a glimpse of the street outside. Reese stopped. Her mother's car was parked on the road. Reese must have walked right past it on her way in. Had she been in the car? Was she sitting in there for some reason? Maybe she just got back from somewhere?

Reese went to the window and peered out. It didn't look as though there was anyone in the car, but she might be lying down.

She went through the rest of the house, making sure her mother wasn't lying on her bed, or perhaps sick and locked in the bathroom, but there was no sign of her. Reese didn't like the strange, slightly sick sensation in her stomach. Something felt really off, like when she'd had a fight with someone, or when she read something horrible on the internet, or knew she needed to do something she was going to dread. She was being stupid. Her mum had only gone out and forgotten her phone. Nothing bad had happened. She'd be back within the next hour, maybe with Tyler, with him probably moaning 'cause she hadn't brought the car, and then things would be normal again.

Reese distracted herself by grabbing a drink and a snack from the fridge and then scrolling through her phone for a while. She did forget about her mother's strange disappearance for a bit, too, getting caught up in some relationship drama—other people's not hers—because one of the boys had decided to stop 'talking' to one of her friends and was going to start talking to another girl instead.

The front door clicked open, and Reese jumped to her feet. "Mum?"

Her brother's voice came back to her. "No, it's me."

"Isn't Mum with you?"

"Why would she be?"

"I thought she might have come to pick you up."

He frowned at her. "Duh, her car is parked outside."

"I know. I thought maybe she'd walked to meet you."

He wrinkled his nose, looking at her like he thought she was stupid, which he probably did. "Why would she do that?"

Reese wasn't going to get into an argument with him about why their mother might go to pick him up from school. "The point is, I don't know where she is, and she hasn't got her phone with her."

"So? She might have just gone to the shops or something."

"But why hasn't taken her phone?"

They could always get hold of her, no matter what. That was why Reese was worrying so much. She couldn't remember a time when she hadn't been able to have her mother on hand.

"I think I'm going to call Dad."

She picked up her phone again, but Tyler rolled his eyes. "Seriously, he's at work. He's *busy*. He's not going to want you phoning him 'cause Mum's gone to the shops and forgot her phone. Get real, Reese."

She chewed her lower lip, considering what he'd said. Dad was busy—too busy to even come home to them during the week now. She would feel stupid if she bothered him and interrupted a meeting or something, only for their mum to walk through the door.

Dad will come back home again if Mum is missing.

The idea felt strange inside her, like she knew she wasn't supposed to think such things but couldn't help prodding and poking it, finding out how it felt. Would their dad *have* to come back then? Would he have to give up his job and then they wouldn't have to move? Guilt washed over her. Was she really thinking that something happening to her mum was worth staying in Bristol? What kind of person was she?

"Okay, fine. We'll wait a bit and see if she shows up."

"I'm sure she will. She's probably bumped into someone and gone to have a cup of tea or something."

Tyler headed to the fridge and opened it, sticking his head in to look for food. His nonchalance was making her think that perhaps she was overreacting, but then Tyler didn't seem to get bothered by much at all. As long as he got fed, got enough sleep, and played football, Tyler was content. Reese wished she could live life as simply. She felt like she overthought everything, from the way she said 'hello' to someone she saw in the street, to if she'd posted the right photo to Instagram. She was constantly worried about what people thought of her.

Now those worries seemed stupid. She had a very real concern. This had been a culmination of how she'd been feeling all week, that sense that something wasn't quite right. The disturbed nights had left her tired and irritable, and now her mum was missing, it felt like she'd almost been waiting for something like this to happen.

Tyler grabbed his snack and took it up to his bedroom, leaving Reese alone downstairs. She took her phone into the living room and put the TV on, trying to distract herself. Her mum would be home any minute now, probably complaining she'd forgotten her phone. Reese didn't really watch what was on TV, scrolling through her phone instead. She didn't even properly focus on that, a part of her constantly listening out for the front door opening.

The time approached six p.m., and her mother still wasn't home. They normally had dinner by six-thirty, and that nothing was being prepared and they'd had no message to say to help themselves alarmed her even more.

Reese went upstairs and opened her brother's bedroom door.

"Hey," he protested, "ever heard of knocking?"

She ignored him. "Mum's still not home, and it's almost dinnertime. I'm really worried now. I'm going to call Dad."

He sat up on his bed. "So, there's no dinner?"

"Oi, dickhead, focus on the important part. Mum's still not home. Something must have happened."

"Do you think we can order pizza then?"

Reese rolled her eyes. "God, you can be such a twat sometimes."

"You're the twat."

She scowled and shut the door on him. She didn't have the energy to get into a fight with her stupid little brother right now.

She went back downstairs and grabbed her phone. Then she scrolled until she reached her dad's number and hit 'call'. Her stomach cramped with nerves. Was she nervous calling her dad, or just nervous about what the result would be? If he said everything was fine, and that she didn't need to worry, would she be calmed by his reassurances or annoyed that no one was taking this seriously? But if he got worried as well, she'd have to face that something had actually happened.

"Hello, sweetheart. It's not like you to call me."

Another stab of guilt. Was she a bad daughter? But she felt better just hearing his voice, like she was handing her concerns over to someone responsible.

"Yeah, sorry, Dad. I am calling for a reason."

"Is everything all right?"

"Not really. Mum wasn't here when I got back from school, and she's left her phone here so I can't get hold of her."

"Oh." He paused for a moment. "Did she mention that she had to go anywhere?"

"No, not that I can remember."

"Check the calendar in the kitchen. She might have written an appointment on it."

Reese went into the kitchen and checked. "No, there's nothing on it."

"Hmm. That doesn't mean she didn't have one, though."

"But, Dad, the car is still parked outside. Where would she have gone and not taken the car?" She suddenly thought of something else. "And the front door wasn't locked when I got home. She wouldn't have gone out and not locked the front door."

"Maybe she left it open for you? She might have thought you'd forgotten your key."

"Why would she have thought that?"

Irritation filled his tone. "I don't know, Reese, I'm thinking out loud, okay? You've only just thrown this at me, and I'm running through every possibility."

"Sorry," she said, her voice small. A lump constricted her throat, and hot tears burned her eyes. She hadn't expected her dad to get angry with her. It wasn't as though this was her fault.

He must have sensed her reaction. "No, I'm sorry, love. You don't have anything to be sorry about. Look, I'm supposed to be having a business dinner tonight, and I need to be there in," he paused, and she assumed he was checking his watch, "forty-five minutes. Give your mum another couple of hours, and if she's still not home by the time I've finished my meal, I'll drive back up to Bristol, okay?"

"Okay."

"Are you both hungry? I assume your brother is home?"

"Yes, he is."

"I'll order you both pizza. Don't worry, you won't go hungry."

She gave a sigh. "That's not what I'm worried about, Dad. I'm worried about Mum."

"I'm sure there's a perfectly reasonable explanation. I'll have my phone on me in case you need to get hold of me, and if she shows up, send me a text."

"I will."

"Bye, love."

"Bye," she said and ended the call.

She sniffed and wiped her eyes and wished her dad had said he was dropping everything and coming up to Bristol right away. Sometimes it did feel as though he put his job before everything else. They were having to sell the house and move to a whole different city, and leave their school and friends behind, all because he'd started a new job, and now Mum was missing, and he was going off to a work dinner instead of rushing home to look after his kids. Okay, she knew she was fifteen now and more than old enough to take care of herself and Tyler for a few hours, but that was hardly the point. Something had happened, and he knew she was upset, but he still chose to go out to dinner.

She kept going to pick up the phone to call her mum and then having to remind herself that her mum's phone was still sitting on the coffee table where she'd found it.

The doorbell rang, and she hurried to answer it, a stupid little part of her hoping it would be Mum, and the other part fearful it would be the police standing on the doorstep, their stern but sympathetic faces making it obvious they had bad news to impart, but instead it was the bloke from Domino's. The poor guy had probably never had anyone so disappointed to receive their pizza order before. She almost felt bad for him.

She thanked him and carried the pizza into the lounge. No one was here to tell them to eat at the dining room table, so they could eat on their laps in front of the TV instead. Their dad had obviously been feeling guilty, as he'd got them all the sides as well as a meat-laden pizza.

"Tyler," she called up the stairs. "Food."

Her brother raced down and saw the pizza and chicken wings and cookies. "Ah, nice one. Mum should go missing more often."

Reese slapped him across the back of the head.

"Hey," he protested, "what was that for?"

"Don't say stuff like that. Mum could be lying in a hospital bed or worse for all we know."

He stared at her, and then his lower lip wobbled. He suddenly looked younger than he was—like he had when he was eight or nine. "You don't think that, do you?"

She let out a sigh, wondering if she'd been too harsh on him. "I don't know what to think. Come on, let's put on a film and eat our pizza. Dad's going to come home if Mum hasn't shown up in a couple of hours."

That seemed to placate him. "Okay."

Reese sat down to eat her pizza and prayed her mum would be okay.

Chapter Thirty-Three

A couple of hours had passed, and there was still no sign of their mother. Their film had finished, and they'd eaten all the pizza, so now Reese and Tyler sat in silence, scrolling through their phones. Reese's worry was a twisted knot of anxiety in her stomach. She had no doubt that something terrible had happened.

Reese got back on her phone and called her dad. To her frustration, it went straight through to answerphone. She left a message. "Dad, she's still not home. I hope you're on your way back now."

"Maybe he's driving," Tyler suggested.

"He has a phone attachment in his car. It's not like he couldn't answer it."

"He might have been in a rush, and he forgot to put it in the holder."

Reese thought her brother was giving their dad too much credit. Their dad was so caught up in work, it was like he had blinkers on and nothing else mattered. She knew his job was important, but was it really more important than the rest of their family? As far as she'd been concerned, they'd been getting on just fine before he'd applied for the new job, and simply because he had ambitions, they all had to change their whole lives. Their mum said it would mean they'd have more money around and could go on all-inclusive holidays and buy nice clothes and live in a better area, but Reese didn't care about all that stuff if it meant she wasn't going to be able to hang out with her friends. She told herself that she'd move back up to Bristol as soon as she was old enough to, but that felt like ages away, and in the meantime, she'd have to start over.

Her phone rang, and she snatched it up, hoping her mum would be on the end of the line. Instead, she saw 'Dad' on the screen.

"Hi," she said as she answered. "Did you listen to my message? Mum's still not back."

"Yes, love, I heard. My meeting ran over, but I'm leaving now, okay?"

She let out a breath of frustration. "So, you're still going to be at least an hour and a half?"

"Yes, around then. I'll be there as soon as I can. Try not to worry."

The call ended, and Reese tightened her fingers around the phone, resisting the urge to throw it across the room. Breaking it wasn't going to help anyone, and it would only make it harder for their parents to get in touch with her.

She glanced over at Tyler who sat on the sofa with his knees pulled into his chest. She couldn't remember a time when the two of them had sat in a room together. Normally, they'd both vanish off to their own bedrooms, but she got the sense now that neither of them wanted to be alone.

"Maybe I should start calling around the hospitals," she said, thinking that was the sort of thing she'd seen people doing on TV shows. "She could have been in an accident."

Tyler chewed at his lower lip. "You don't think she might have...done something? Do you?"

"Done something?" It took a moment to understand what he meant. "You mean kill herself?"

He shrugged awkwardly. "I don't know. Well, yes, that is what I mean."

"She wouldn't do that."

"How do you know? She's been really stressed out and unhappy lately. You must have noticed. She got all weird about those stupid boxes, remember?"

"Yeah, she's stressed, but she's not suicidal."

"Maybe we should have done more to help her around the house with Dad gone."

To Reese's horror, tears shimmered in her brother's eyes. "Jesus, Tyler, she's not killed herself because we didn't bring our dishes down to the kitchen."

He sniffled. "But it's everything else, too. Moving house and Dad being away. Maybe it all got too much for her."

"Shut up," she snapped. "She has not killed—"

From somewhere upstairs came a muffled thud.

They both fell quiet and lifted their gazes to the ceiling.

"Did you hear that?" Tyler asked.

"Duh, yeah, I think the neighbours would have heard that."

"What was it? You don't think...?"

He shook his head. "We checked upstairs. She wasn't up there."

Reese frowned. Could she have been hiding? Maybe in one of the wardrobes or under a bed? "I think we need to look again."

"Together?" he checked.

"I'm not going up there on my own."

Tyler nodded, and they both got to their feet and left the room. Reese led the way, and they climbed the stairs to the first floor.

"Mum?" Reese called. "Are you up here?"

This was crazy. There was no way her mum would have been hiding upstairs for hours. She would have known how worried they'd be, and why would she do it in the first place? She wasn't a toddler in a game of hide and seek.

But Reese had heard something, hadn't she? They both had. If it hadn't been their mum, who—or what—was it?

Reese glanced to the ceiling and spotted the loft hatch. She thought to where the stack of boxes had been before—right underneath it. Had someone knocked them down when they'd tried to climb up? Her breath caught in her chest, her heart thundering. This was insane. Maybe she should call the police? But if she was wrong, they'd think she was a crazy person. Mentally, she battled with herself. Mum was missing, so she could report that. They were technically two minors who'd been left alone. She could lead with that with the police and then mention the loft.

"What are you thinking?" Tyler asked.

"That we should call the police now."

"Dad'll be here soon. Let's just wait for him."

"What if she's up there?" She raised her eyes towards the loft hatch.

He screwed up his nose. "Why would she be up there?"

"Because we don't know where she is, and I think that noise came from in there, and do you remember when all the boxes fell down during the night? They were right under the loft, remember?"

"You're saying Mum knocked them down trying to climb into the loft?"

"No, dummy. I'm saying someone else knocked them down climbing into the loft and now maybe they'd taken Mum up there with them."

His eyebrows shot up his forehead. "You can't be serious. There's probably just a pigeon got stuck up there or something."

Immediately, she felt like an idiot. Talk about jumping to conclusions. Of course that was all it was—some bird got stuck up there, or maybe even a bat. She'd been watching too many horror films. Her cheeks heated at the thought of her calling the police and telling them someone had taken their mother into the attic and them doing a search and finding a bird.

She wished her dad would hurry up so someone else could take over from the decisions. She didn't like having to be the responsible one when she had no idea what she was supposed to do.

"Okay, fine. Let's go back downstairs and just wait for Dad. He'll only be another hour or so, I hope."

She prayed the car didn't break down, or he didn't hit traffic. There was no reason why he should, since it was hardly rush hour—unless there was an accident—and his car was a brand-new one that came with his job, so it should be reliable. Even so, she felt as though anything that could go wrong, probably would.

The two of them went back down to the lounge and resumed their positions on the sofa. Reese checked her phone and went through all her social media accounts, willing time away.

Tyler got to his feet.

"Where are you going?" Reese asked.

"Up to my room."

A knot tightened in her stomach. "No, we should stay together."

He stared at her. "Well, I still need to go upstairs."

"Why?"

"I want to go to the toilet."

"So use the downstairs one," she said in exasperation.

"I need to take a shit. I'm not doing that while you can hear everything I do."

"Jesus Christ." She rolled her eyes. "Fine."

Tyler left the room, and she heard his feet on the stairs, followed by the click of the bathroom door closing.

She waited for him. He probably had his phone in there with him and was using it as a social event rather than something he just needed to get done. She'd never understood the enjoyment of sitting in a room that stinks of your own shit for any longer than was physically necessary. Her dad was the same as her brother and disappeared in there for ages. Maybe it was a male thing, though she suspected her dad only did it to get away from the rest of them for a while.

She didn't like sitting down here on her own. She paced to the window and watched out on the street for any sign of her dad arriving. Every time headlights illuminated the road, her heart leapt with hope, only for those hopes to be dashed a moment later when the car continued past the house and vanished around the corner.

With a sigh, she went to the bottom of the stairs and called up them, "Tyler, are you done yet?"

He didn't reply but if he was on his phone, watching TikToks or something, he wouldn't have heard her. She stomped back up the stairs.

"Tyler, seriously, it doesn't take this long to have a shit." She wasn't going to admit to him that she didn't like being on her own. She was the older sister and was practically an adult now.

She stopped outside the bathroom door and froze. It was open a crack. "Tyler?"

No sound came from inside. If he was watching stuff on his phone, she would have heard him by now. Had he gone to his room instead? But no, that door was wide open, and there was no sign of him, and why wouldn't he answer her?

Despite her needing him to hear her, she found herself lowering her voice, so it was barely above a whisper. "Tyler? What are you doing?"

She reached out, the tips of her fingers skirting the wood of the door, and she pushed lightly. The door opened, but not fully, hitting on something behind it.

She suddenly understood what was going on, and her fear turned to anger. "Tyler, I know you're going to jump out at me and try and scare me. That's not funny, you know, with Mum missing and everything."

Reese waited for him to emerge around the side of the door, his hands held up in a 'you got me' stance, but nothing happened. "Tyler?"

She pushed at the door again, harder than was really necessary, and then, when she hit him with it and he didn't yell out, she stuck her head around the corner.

Reese screamed.

Tyler was lying facedown on the bathroom floor, his legs blocking the doorway. Blood coated his back.

Oh God, oh God, oh God.

She dropped to her knees in the cramped space, putting her hand on his shoulder. Her mind was a blur of overthinking, trying to figure out what had happened. Had he hit himself somehow? Was he still alive? Where the hell was his phone—it never went far from him? Shit, she'd left hers downstairs. Stupid, stupid, stupid. She needed to call an ambulance.

"I'll be back in one minute, okay, Tyler. You're going to be all right." She had no idea if that was true, but she couldn't bring herself to think that her little brother might actually be dead. They weren't exactly close, but she'd never even thought about living in a world where Tyler wasn't in it. She'd always taken his constant presence for granted.

A noise came from outside, footsteps, creaking a floorboard directly outside the bathroom. Oh, thank God, her dad must have got here already.

"Dad, Tyler's hurt," she called out. "He needs help."

She rose to her feet, her back still to the door.

A hand clamped over her mouth, stifling her breath, and she screamed against a cold, clammy palm.

Chapter Thirty-Four

The search warrant had come in for the Ford Transit, and SOCO were there now, working on the vehicle. One thing that hadn't been found was anything indicating where Sweeny was now.

Ryan had requested that uniformed officers go to each of the addresses that they'd narrowed down from the original list. The houses in the same area the van had been found, and those with families, had been prioritised. Officers had been instructed to check on the families and request permission to search the house for anyone who shouldn't be there, but so far, he hadn't heard that they'd found anything or anyone.

He couldn't decide if he wanted to be right about his theory that they'd find Sweeny holed up in one of his client's houses, or wrong. If he was wrong, it meant they were back to square one as far as finding him went, but if he was right...

That part almost didn't bear thinking about.

Linda approached his desk. "Boss, the control desk has just had a call come from a Mr Andy Bolton. His wife wasn't home when his children got back from school, and they've been worried. He was working down in Exeter but is driving back up because of the missing wife, only now he says he can't get hold of either of the children. They're not answering their mobile phones or the house phone, and he's understandably worried. Anyway, I ran the address through the system, and it's one of the ones we have on our list. It's on the market, and Philip Sweeny went there to film a virtual tour."

"Is the house in Lawrence Hill?"

She shook her head. "No, Whitehall."

"Shit. Right next door. He must have parked the van and walked the rest. How old are the children?"

"Twelve and fifteen."

"Similar ages to the Wyndham family," he said. "We need to get a patrol car over there, whoever is closest. Let them know the family's lives could be in danger, but that Philip Sweeny is considered dangerous." Ryan got to his feet. "I need to go and see Superintendent Symth and request an Armed Response Unit immediately."

Chapter Thirty-Five

S omething wet and warm soaked into her clothes.

Something was very wrong.

Helen's first thought was that she'd wet the bed and it was urine, but as she gradually came around, she realised she wasn't in her bed. Hard boards supported her body.

Pain bloomed hot and bright, snatching her breath. She was hurt! Panic followed quickly after. That wasn't urine she felt but blood.

It all suddenly came back to her: how she'd come up to the loft looking for boxes, only to find someone else up here. He'd hurt her—badly—stabbed her in the stomach, she thought, but what had happened next, she had no idea.

Oh God, where were the kids? She had no idea what time it was, but she could no longer see daylight peeping through the tiny slats between the roof tiles. The kids had been due home not long after she'd climbed into the loft.

Was he still in here with her?

It was difficult to hear anything above her own wheezing breath and the slow thud of blood through her ears. What damage had he caused with the knife? She'd lost a lot of blood, that was why she felt so woozy and why she couldn't get herself to wake up properly. Had he punctured her intestine? Was an injury like that fatal? Did he think she was dead? She managed to open her eyes, but it was only darkness around her.

If the man was still in the loft with her, he must know she wasn't dead. Was he waiting for her to die? If she moved, would he stab her again? The thought terrified her, but what scared her even more was the thought that he wasn't in here with her and had gone down to kill her children.

Reese. Tyler.

They were all alone. Their dad was in Exeter, and she was up here. Did they have any idea what had happened to her? Had they come looking for her and he'd stabbed them, too? The possibility of her children being dead made her want to give in to her injuries. What would be the point in fighting if they were gone? Her life would be over.

As her eyes grew used to the darkness—helped along by the few slats of moonlight peeping between the tiles, which made her think that they could do with some work being done on the roof, a crazed thought considering her current situation—she dared to look around. It was too dark to see anything in detail, but she was able to make out the dark block of the chimney breast. The swathes of spiders' webs were invisible in the gloom, but she knew they were there, as were the wooden struts holding up the roof. How far away was the loft hatch? Did she have enough strength to crawl over and then be able to lower it and release the ladder? Such a simple thing seemed like a monumental task—like she was being asked to climb Mount Everest or skydive—but she had no choice. Her children were in danger, and she wasn't just going to lie here and give up when they needed her.

Helen tried to push herself to all fours, but her limbs didn't want to comply. Her whole body trembled, but she managed to get herself onto her elbows and she commando crawled towards the hatch. She let out a gasp of pain with every movement. The wound in her stomach dragged against the floor, and though she couldn't see it, she knew she was leaving behind a trail of blood like a slug would leave slime. That was how she felt now—sluglike, barely human. She was running on the purely instinctual drive of a mother who needed to save her children. Her life didn't matter. All she wanted was for them to be safe, but a dread deep in her gut that had nothing to do with the stab wound had her believing that they weren't. Would she know if they were dead? She'd carried them both inside her for nine months each, physically joined as though they were one person. Was that sickening dread her body's way of telling her that the biggest parts of her no longer existed?

A wave of pain blackened the edges of her vision, and she curled her fingers into the wood and froze, her breath trapped in her lungs, willing herself to stay conscious. To her relief, the moment passed, and she was able to move again.

The folding ladder sat in front of the hatch. Beyond the metal bars of the ladder, there was a catch on the wooden panel of the loft hatch that she could twist and would open it. That was how he'd been letting himself in and out, opening the loft and lowering himself down onto their landing. He must have been pulling the ladder down to get back up. Why hadn't she heard it? Then she remembered the stacks of boxes and how they'd moved and then toppled. No, he hadn't needed to use the ladder each time. He'd climbed onto the boxes and got up that way.

Somewhere in the house, a phone was ringing. On and on, but no one answered it. Did it go unanswered because no one was home, or because someone was stopping them?

She knew there was no way she had enough strength to lower the ladder, and even if she did, her body's coordination wouldn't comply enough to navigate her way down it.

She gritted her teeth and twisted the catch. What should be such a simple thing had become like a mountain to climb. To her relief, it turned, and gravity did the rest of the work, the hatch dropping open.

Light from the landing blinded her, and she squinted and twisted her face away, allowing her eyes to get used to the light. She turned back. Could she hear anyone? See anyone? She listened hard. If the children were already dead, she wouldn't be able to hear them. The thought tightened her throat and made it hard to breathe. She resisted calling their names, knowing it would tell the man who'd been hiding in their loft that she was still alive. He might already know—could be waiting just out of sight, ready to finish the job.

She needed to get down there.

Helen couldn't allow herself to think too hard about what needed to happen next. It was going to hurt—hurt worse than anything she was feeling now, and her current level of pain was easily a ten out of ten. The only pain she'd known that had come anything close to this was when she'd given birth to Reese, and though she'd been begging for an epidural, the nurses had told her the anaesthetist was busy with an emergency and wouldn't be able to help her. She remembered becoming almost animalistic then, lowing like a cow in a field, sucking on the gas and air and insisting it wasn't doing anything.

That had been bad, but what she was about to do would be worse.

Just do it!

Her only other choice was to stay here and die, and that didn't seem like much of a choice at all.

Helen wasn't going to go headfirst, though. She didn't want to break her neck. It hurt, but she managed to bring herself around, so her feet stuck over the hole. From that position, she wriggled backwards, her feet hanging down, followed by her shins and knees, then her thighs. She pictured the man who'd stabbed her standing below, ready to grab her ankles and drag her the rest of the way.

She reached the point where she was folded at a right angle, the edge of the hatch pressing the wound in her stomach. The agony was intense. She couldn't stay in this position, or she *would* pass out. She used her arms to push herself up, straightening her body. She teetered on the edge and then pushed again and dropped the distance between the ceiling and the floor.

Sickening pain and a hot flash of nausea followed by a wave of cold. Nothing quite felt stable around her, the landing tipping and tilting. Her last thoughts before she lost consciousness were her children's names.

Chapter Thirty-Six

Ryan put his foot down, following the Armed Response Unit to the address they had for the Bolton family. Aware Sweeny was most likely armed with a knife and unafraid to use it, he and Mallory had donned body armour before setting out.

He drove as fast as he dared, his heart thudding, his vision sharp and clear. There wasn't much traffic on the road this evening, so they made progress quickly.

They reached the correct street. It was a wide road with new build, detached houses on either side. Already, the pulsing light of the initial response car filled the gloaming sky. The uniformed officers were creating an outer and inner cordon to keep the public away from the house. An ambulance had been called in on standby, too, but Ryan prayed they weren't going to need to use it.

People emerged from their homes, pale-faced and worried, but also enjoying a bit of excitement on the street. Uniformed police shouted at them to stay inside their homes, sweeping them back with their arms, but they were reluctant to miss the entertainment. Cars attempting to drive down the road from either end were stopped, and the drivers and passengers climbed out, craning their necks to get a view at what was happening.

The armed officers moved quickly, surrounding the house. They would go at the signal, gaining entry any way they could, be that through doors or windows.

"Any sign of life from inside?" Ryan asked the responding officer.

The other man shook his head. "No. We haven't seen any movement. The house has been in darkness since we got here a few minutes ago."

Ryan was handed a loudspeaker. He switched it on and turned to face the front of the property. He would try to strike up communication first, but he didn't plan on giving it long.

"Philip Sweeny, we have you surrounded." His amplified voice cut through the rest of the hubbub of the street. "If you can hear me, come to a window and make yourself known. We don't want anyone else hurt."

People might already be injured or worse inside the house, and he wasn't going to give Sweeny any opportunity to harm anyone else.

No response came. The house remained dark.

They couldn't wait any longer.

He gave the signal for the armed response officers to move in.

They did so with speed and noise, giving warning shouts to Sweeny. Wood splintered and glass smashed, and the whole of the street held its collective breath.

Ryan waited with the air trapped in his chest, poised for the sound of gunfire. The armed police had guns, but they were trained to use their Tasers rather than shoot if they were able to.

A call came through on the radio.

"Three people down. One adult and two children. We need paramedics in here. No immediate sign of Sweeny."

Ryan wanted to roar with fury. He was too late. Sweeny had attacked another innocent family and got away with it. "He likes to hide," he said over the radio. "Make sure he's not in the loft or hidden somewhere else in the house."

As soon as they got the wounded out of the house and to safety, the officers would do a slow methodical search of the entire home, including the loft space.

From farther down the road came a flurry of activity. A male voice shouted. "That's my house! Those are my family." The father had arrived.

"Keep him back," Ryan instructed.

If the man's entire family was dead, he would be unpredictable. They didn't need him getting involved right now. There would be plenty of time for interviews later, if he was in any state to give one.

Paramedics entered the building, and Ryan found his hand cupped over his mouth. Maybe he should get in there, but he just couldn't face it. One of the victims was a girl, and that he'd failed her cut deep.

A voice came over the radio again. "We've got two alive, one dead on scene."

Ryan shook his head and turned away. Maybe he should be happy that two of the family had survived, but even one loss of life was one too many.

"You did everything you could," Mallory said from beside him. "This wasn't your fault."

Despite uniforms' attempt to get people to stay in their houses, a decent-sized crowd had still formed. It looked as though the neighbours were having a goddamned lawn party.

One man caught his eye, sitting on the doorstep of a house farther down, on the opposite side of the road. He was long-limbed, with fair hair and the kind of bland face that would be hard to describe in a lineup.

Ryan's stomach lurched.

It was him. The son of a bitch had wanted to watch the fallout, or perhaps he'd been waiting for the father to come home so he could find his family stabbed.

"There!" Ryan shouted. "Sweeny's over there."

Sweeny realised he'd been spotted and jumped to his feet.

Ryan had no intention of letting him get away again. He ran for the outer cordon and leapt over it. He was barely aware of Mallory shouting his name.

Sweeny vanished between two houses, and Ryan took after him. He remembered his radio and, barely breaking his pace, used it to inform the other officers which direction Sweeny had gone.

Sweeny ran down the side of the house, knocking over a wheely bin. The bin fell into Ryan's path, forcing him to leap over it. Ahead of him, Sweeny reached a wooden fence, and he hooked his hands over the top and pulled himself up and over. Sweeny was tall and agile, and Ryan hoped he'd be able to keep up.

His colleagues were close behind.

Ryan used his radio again. "He's gone westbound over the fence, backing onto Waring Road. Cut him off."

He reached the fence Sweeny had hauled himself over and jumped for it.

"Jesus Christ," he muttered, and groaned as he yanked himself up, his biceps and shoulder muscles straining. For a moment, he didn't think he was going to make it, and he'd fall to the ground again, but somehow, he managed to hook his chest over the top of the fence. That gave him enough leverage to pull the rest of his body over.

He hoped his colleagues were moving faster.

Clumsily, he jumped to the ground on the other side and gave himself a second to get his bearing. The red-brick wall of the house ran to his right-hand side, but he couldn't see Sweeny.

"Fuck."

Ryan kept going.

A figure stepped out from behind the back wall of the house and punched him hard and low in the stomach.

Sweeny.

Ryan folded in half, confused. Though Sweeny turned and ran the moment after he'd struck Ryan, it felt as though he hadn't removed his fist from Ryan's gut. But then he realised it wasn't his fist embedded in his stomach but the handle of a knife. Sweeny had got him right underneath his body armour.

Shit.

His knees gave way, and he fell to all fours. He was barely aware of someone running behind him.

"Oh God, Ryan."

Mallory.

She opened her mouth and shouted, "Officer down! DI Chase is down. We need an ambulance right away."

"He went that way."

Ryan put one hand around the blade that was still embedded in his stomach, the warm pulse of blood seeping between his fingers. His instinct was to pull it out again, but his training kicked in and he knew not to. Doing so would only make the blood loss worse. He managed to lift his other hand and point in the direction Sweeny had gone.

"It's okay," Mallory reassured him, yanking off her jacket. "We've got every officer in Bristol hunting him down. He's not getting away."

"He'd better not," Ryan managed to growl.

Mallory bundled the jacket into a ball and surrounded the hilt of the knife with the material, pressing down firmly to help staunch the bleeding. The pain was overwhelming, taking over his thoughts completely. Was he going to die? Was this it for him? Regret washed over him for all the things he hadn't done. Who was going to take care of Donna now? He hadn't wanted her to go through her cancer treatment alone.

One thought in particular was bright and clear: would he see Hayley again?

The paramedics had been forced to come from the back way, unable to just climb over a fence as Ryan had done.

"Give us some space, please," the female half of the paramedic team said to Mallory. "We'll take over from here." She addressed Ryan. "It's DI Chase, isn't it?"

"Ryan," he managed to croak.

Someone who was about to help save his life definitely got to call him by his first name.

"Okay, Ryan. We're going to get you to the hospital, okay? You're going to need surgery, but you're going to be all right. We'll take care of you now."

"I'm coming, too," Mallory announced.

The paramedics must have known better than to argue with her.

Chapter Thirty-Seven

Mallory was curled up in a chair at Ryan's bedside, drifting in and out of sleep, lulled by the rhythmical beeping of the machines attached to him. He'd got through the surgery without any complication, and for that she was grateful.

She hadn't told Donna yet. She knew the other woman was going through enough on her own, and since they were divorced, it wasn't as though Donna was Ryan's next of kin anymore. Ryan wouldn't have wanted Donna to weaken her immune system further by a sleepless night.

She'd had no choice but to ask her parents to stay with Ollie overnight. It had been difficult for her, letting go of some of that responsibility, but she hadn't wanted Ryan to wake up and find no one here. She remembered how she'd been dreaming of having a night away from home to get a restful night's sleep, but this wasn't exactly what she'd had in mind.

The grey light of morning peeped through the slats in the window blind. It was just after seven. She stifled a yawn and thought about caffeine. She was going to need it even more to get through today.

From the hospital bed came a groan.

Mallory sat forward, suddenly wide awake. "Ryan?"

His eyes opened, and he winced. "I feel like shit."

She couldn't help but smile. "I'm not surprised. The surgeons removed a four-inch blade from your abdomen."

"Did it...?" He paused as though the effort of speaking had suddenly become too much. "Did it go okay?"

"No complications. The doctors will be around shortly to speak to you, though."

He seemed to sink into the pillow at the news. "Good. That's good."

"I'd say you were lucky, but I'm guessing you don't feel very lucky right now."

"No, not really." His eyes slipped shut again.

He was on a morphine drip for the pain, and she assumed the drugs and anaesthesia plus the blood loss had done a number on his system. He would be needing to sleep a lot over the following days and weeks so he could recover.

She thought he was going to go back to sleep again, but then his eyes opened.

"Did they catch him?" he asked, his voice croaky. "Did they get Sweeny?"

"Yes. Not far from where he stabbed you. He's in custody now."

"What about the family? Did they—?"

Mallory bit her lower lip. "The two children, Tyler and Reese, survived, though, like you, they both suffered stab wounds. The mother, Helen, didn't make it."

His eyes closed again. "Fuck. If only we'd got there sooner."

"We did everything we could. Sweeny attacked the mother in the loft sometime yesterday afternoon and held her there. She'd lost a lot of blood. It looks as though she threw herself out of the loft hatch to try and save the kids."

"I hope she knew they'd survived before she died. Dying while believing your kids are dead must be the worst thing in the world."

"She made it to them before she passed. She crawled across the landing and found them. The girl, Reese, was conscious enough to know what was happening, she said, and held her mother as she died."

"Poor kid."

"Yeah, it's not really the sort of thing you can get over. The father arrived shortly after we did. I imagine he's going to be blaming himself as well for not getting back sooner. Apparently, he went to a business dinner after work, even though he knew the mother was missing."

Ryan's shake of the head was so slight it was barely noticeable. "I was like that, too. Put work before everything else. Maybe now he'll realise how lucky he is to have two children who are still alive."

MALLORY LEFT THE HOSPITAL mid-morning, swapping with Donna who Mallory had insisted needed to be told, despite Ryan's protests not to bother his ex-wife. It had taken her pointing out to him that Donna would be furious *not* to be told that had made him relent.

Now she was home, and she wanted a hot shower and a decent cup of tea and to get her head down for a couple of hours.

"I'm home!" she called as she opened the front door and threw her keys down on the hall console.

She headed into the kitchen to discover her parents sitting at the kitchen table, both with a mug of tea in front of them. There was a third one, which she assumed was meant for her, or perhaps it was for Ollie, though he didn't normally like hot drinks. Tension simmered in the air.

"Everything all right?" she asked.

Her mother grimaced. "You might want to go and see your brother. He's upset about something."

She stared at them. "You didn't think to go and see him yourself?"

"He doesn't want to talk to us, and you know what he can get like. Once he's made up his mind about something, he digs his heels in like a stubborn mule."

She'd been hoping to sit down for five minutes, but that clearly wasn't going to happen. Neither of her parents had even bothered to ask how her day had gone. That she'd helped to apprehend a murderer and had spent the night at her boss's bedside in hospital obviously hadn't computed with them. Sometimes, even though they'd handed Ollie's care over to her, it felt as though they still didn't see her as a fully functioning adult with a life of her own.

"Oh-kay," she drew out the word, "I'll go and ask Ollie, shall I?"

She went upstairs to her brother's bedroom. Ollie had his back to her and was leaning over a small suitcase on his bed.

"What are you doing, Ollie?"

He didn't turn around but picked up another piece of clothing from a pile he had next to the case and put it on top of the last one. "I'm going."

"Where are you going?"

"To live somewhere else."

"Why?"

"Because I hurt you, Mallory. I heard Mum and Dad talking, and they said I hit you."

He'd put a couple of his favourite tops into the case, together with his favourite book. The sight of them broke her heart.

"You didn't hit me, Ollie. We had an accident while you were having a bad dream, that's all. I know you'd never hurt me."

His shoulders shook, and she realised he was crying. She put her hands on his shoulders, turned him around, and hugged him hard.

"Now unpack your stuff. I don't want you going anywhere. You're stuck with me, okay?"

"Okay, Mallory. I'm sorry."

"You don't have anything to be sorry about."

She left him putting his stuff back in his drawers and stormed downstairs. It had been an incredibly long day, and her emotions had already gone through the wringer, and now she had this to deal with as well. Sometimes, it really did feel as though it was all too much to deal with, but that didn't mean she was going to give up on her brother.

"You told Ollie that he hurt me?" she blurted as she walked back into the kitchen.

"No, sweetheart, we didn't," her mother said, "at least not intentionally. We were talking about everything between ourselves, and he overheard us."

"You should have been more careful! Ollie thinks he needs to move out now. He thinks he's a danger to me."

Her parents exchanged a glance.

Her father lifted a hand towards her face. "Come on, love. What about your eye? You look like you've gone ten rounds with Mike Tyson."

"Don't exaggerate. I have a dangerous job. I put myself in far more dangerous situations than living with Ollie every single day. My boss ended up in hospital last night because a man who'd already killed five people and injured two others attacked him. I was only seconds away when he was stabbed. It could easily have been me."

Her mother paled. "You're really not helping me feel better."

"It wasn't my intention to make you feel better," she snapped. "You're missing the point. Ollie isn't dangerous. It was just an accident, for goodness' sake."

"You still got hurt. I'm worried about you, Mallory. Ollie is my son, but you're my daughter, and I'm allowed to care about what happens to you, too. This life you're living, it's not...normal."

"Since when have I cared about normal?"

"I'd just like you to go out a bit more, maybe meet someone. It's not like you're getting any younger."

Was her mother seriously going to start giving her a lecture about her biological clock?

"I'm fine, Mum, and I'm only thirty-one. It's not like I'm past it."

Mallory remembered when she'd been in her twenties and had spent almost every weekend at a live concert or at a festival. She couldn't remember the last time she'd been to see a band play. She was different now, and while she couldn't quite bring herself to give up the black hair dye or let her piercings heal over completely, she didn't mind. Sure, seeing all those bands had been fun, but in a way, it had all been empty, too. Her life had meaning now, she had a purpose, and that always beat a few hours in a venue with a thousand people who meant nothing to her.

Her mother sighed. "I know. Forget I said anything."

"If you really want me to have more of a life, maybe you can just help out a bit more?" Mallory suggested.

"You never let us, love," her dad threw in. "Unless you're really desperate because of work, like last night, you tell us you're fine."

She considered that for a moment. As much as she hated to admit it, they weren't wrong. She was always putting across the front that she was coping, even when she wasn't. Ryan could have died last night. What if that had been her, and she'd have had to look back on her life? Would she be happy with what she'd achieved?

"Okay," she relented. "You're right. I will let you help out more. I'm sorry if I've shut you out."

Her mum gazed up at her. "You're a strong woman, Mallory. Your dad and I are both very proud of you."

Mallory's cheeks tweaked in a reluctant smile. "Thanks."

Chapter Thirty-Eight

Reese Bolton looked out of the window of her new bedroom in Exeter, onto the view of the fields beyond. The fleeces of sheep were white dots against the green landscape.

She'd been glad to leave Bristol in the end.

The house still hadn't sold, but that was hardly surprising. Who would want to buy a house where a woman had been murdered and two kids had been stabbed? The life insurance policy her mother had taken out was enough to allow them to move without worrying about selling, so that was what they'd done. Reese was thankful for that, at least. She didn't think she'd have been able to live in that house a moment longer, and it would have been even worse if people had been coming around under the pretence of viewing it, only so they could get a look at where the horror had happened.

She missed her mum every single day. The loss was like a weight in her chest that refused to shift. Over the past few months, she'd discovered grief was a strange thing. She'd have a day or two where she'd almost feel normal, but then she'd be sitting in the car when her dad was driving her to her new school and she'd remember something, and a tight pain closed off her throat and she'd find herself with tears pouring down her face. On those days, her dad noticed and turned around the car and took her home again. Then he'd call into work and say he'd be working from home that day and take her out for a hot chocolate instead.

She'd been so angry with her dad after everything had happened. She'd blamed him for not coming home sooner, but after the initial shock and anger had worn off, she'd realised that no one could blame him more than he blamed himself.

Tyler was suffering just as much as she was. They'd both spent a couple of weeks in hospital, recovering from their injuries, and when he came home, he was a shell of the person he'd been. He withdrew completely, sitting on his bed, barely speaking. His injuries meant he wasn't allowed to play football for at least six weeks, but he said he didn't care and that he didn't want to play anymore. At night, she heard him crying in his bed, and she'd go in and silently slip onto the bed beside him and hug him until his tears stopped and hers began.

At least that bastard, Philip Sweeny, would be going away for life. He'd stabbed a detective who'd come to help them, and the detective had been in hospital at the same time as Tyler and her. When he'd been well enough, he'd come to visit them, and told them how sorry he was about their mother and had apologised for not getting to them sooner. Reese had cried and told him it wasn't his fault, and that he was one of the good guys.

She liked how that sounded. One of the good guys. Someone who protected people against men like Philip Sweeny. It must feel like taking back control again.

Maybe, when she'd finished school, she would become a police officer, too.

Acknowledgements

Huge thanks to everyone who helped to make Chase Down what it is.

Thanks to my editor, Emmy Ellis, for all your encouragement and that dreaded highlighter pen! Thank you to my proofreaders, Tammy Payne, Jacqueline Beard, and Glynis Elliott for helping to spot all those annoying typos!

As always, my gratitude to Patrick O'Donnell for consulting on the book, and all the members of the Cops and Writer's group for answering my many questions.

Special thanks as well to Graham Bartlett for spending some time with me going over British police procedures. Your advice was invaluable, and I will definitely be back for more!

Finally, thanks to you, the reader, for taking the time to read my books.

Until next time,

MK

About the Author

MK Farrar had penned more than ten novels of psychological noir and crime fiction. A British author, she lives in the countryside with her three children and a menagerie of rescue pets.

When she's not writing—which isn't often—she balances out all the murder with baking and binge-watching shows on Netflix.

You can find out more about M K and grab a free book via her website, https://mkfarrar.com

She can also be emailed at mk@mkfarrar.com. She loves to hear from readers!

Also by the Author

DI Erica Swift Thriller
The Eye Thief
The Silent One
The Artisan
The Child Catcher
The Body Dealer
The Gathering Man

Detective Ryan Chase Thriller
Kill Chase
Chase Down

Standalone Psychological Thrillers
Some They Lie
On His Grave
Down to Sleep

Printed in Great Britain
by Amazon